T0354908

Ties That Bind

Ties That Bind

April Williams

Note for Librarians: A cataloguing record for this book is available from Library
and Archives Canada at www.collectionscanada.ca/amicus/index-e.html

Printed in Victoria, BC, Canada.

ISBN: 978-1-4269-1435-5 (sc)
ISBN: 978-1-4269-1434-8 (dj)

Library of Congress Control Number: 2009932572

*Our mission is to efficiently provide the world's finest, most comprehensive book publishing
service, enabling every author to experience success. To find out how to publish your book, your
way, and have it available worldwide, visit us online at www.trafford.com*

Trafford rev. 10/12/2009

 www.trafford.com

North America & international
toll-free: 1 888 232 4444 (USA & Canada)
phone: 250 383 6864 • fax: 812 355 4082

FOR JOYCE P. DAVIS
GONE BUT NEVER FORGOTTEN

ACKNOWLEDGMENTS

To my family, Sherry, Angela, Brent, and Douglas for being supportive and encouraging throughout my life, always sustaining me to always believe in my dreams and follow them to discover just where they may lead.

To Shannon, my best friend from the days we were kids dancing in our elementary school talent show up through the years, you've always been such an endearing friend and never told me what you thought I wanted to hear, just the truth and confidence I needed to see past any obstacles that blocked my path.

There are many others whom have shaped my life in such positive and influential ways throughout the years and to this very day. I thank you all for being there for me.

Taylor Reed seems to embody the lifestyle of a New York socialite, married to a successful New York defense attorney and living in luxury in their upscale high-rise apartment.

Looks can be deceiving and as her life begins to unravel it becomes certain her marriage is in jeopardy and the promise of a brighter future looms in the balance. As her husband, Jonathan struggles to turn their troubled marriage around time and distances proves to cause a rift that may shatter their worlds.

As a handsome young British stranger crosses paths with Taylor in Australia the two suddenly are set on a course of passion and danger. As Jonathan discovers he must place emphasis on his marriage and wife, he senses he may have waited too long and overlooked her one too many times.

Taylor has to make a final decision one which could prove to be fateful or fatal.

About the Author

April Williams was born and raised in Roanoke, Virginia. Her first love of writing began during her senior year of high school when she took a creative writing course, which led her to pursue her dream of writing. She lives with her Shih-Tzu, Dalmao in Virginia working in a therapy office, billing local schools for therapy services. This is her first novel.

CHAPTER 1

PORTRAIT OF THE PAST

O N A cool and crisp winter night, the New York City skyline is luminous and breathtaking from high above the city streets. The multitudes of towering buildings and skyscrapers twinkle in the darkness, shimmering throughout as if stars placed upon land.

Located in a dimly lit, high-rise Manhattan apartment, located on the 21st floor Taylor Reed who is thirty-three years old stands against the vast full length windows of her lavish living room as she gazes down as far as she can see; watching the busy streets below, she hears not a sound as inside her apartment all is still and quiet.

In her boredom and isolation, her mind begins to race thinking of inconsequential and insignificant thoughts, as the outside speeds by unaffected by her presence. Everything appears to be alive and exciting, all the while dead and monotonous within the large apartment.

Gently she presses both palms of her hands against the icy cold glass, watching as with each exhale of her sweet and warm breath the window frosts before her; clouding her view. In a gaze now empty, her eyes no longer shine or shed light on the once vibrant woman she use to be. For all intended purposes those qualities have long since left her; for time, has made changes and set her on a course she did not intend to take.

Her long white satin nightgown drapes along her slender form as her wavy brown hair cascades down her bare back. A sudden chill from the cold window enters her body, causing her to quickly pull away.

As with most evenings, she spends this one alone too, in the apartment she shares with her husband of eleven years; Jonathan Reed. He is one of New York City's most prominent and well sought after defense attorneys. He quickly established himself straight out of college by applying himself with hard work and dedication; with the determination to climb the corporate ladder, with absolutely no intentions of ever turning back.

Over the past few years, Taylor has found herself questioning her life and the direction she now finds herself immersed within. All aspects managed to go in the wrong direction of all she had intended. She concedes if she is to make any sense of her life's journey, she must start at the beginning and move towards the present.

— ◆ —

It was twelve years ago, when Taylor was a senior at Yale. She was planning and mapping out her destiny as all ambitious, young students do. She had it all figured out; obtaining the career, marriage, financial stability, and a family; the picturesque setting of idealistic happiness.

Throughout college, Taylor remained focused and goal oriented, knowing exactly what she wanted in a career; to be an elementary school teacher, just like her mother. She focused on her studies, not allowing anything or anyone to distract her along the way.

Without question, she would not have her dreams not become a reality; a vow she made to herself early on, which in time would prove to be the greatest test in ways she could never have imagined.

It was during her senior year that she formally met the man of her dreams, Jonathan Reed, who happened to be popular, gorgeous, and from an extremely wealthy family. Just three months shy of graduation, their paths finally crossed.

The two had shared several of the same classes. Taylor had taken notice of him instantly; for it was impossible to be within a close proximity and not notice Jonathan, with his muscular and masculine build, wavy dark brown hair that curled as it ran down the back of his neck, and his face with such strong character and elegant chiseled cheekbones, which gave him distinct definition.

His freshly shaven face was youthful and handsome. His most distinctive attribute, his powerful lethal weapon happens to be his seductive and captivating brown eyes. They can easily be expressive enough to talk measures without his mouth having to utter a single word. You can tell just in looking at them if anger or frustration fuels them or if love, warmth or passion drives his gaze.

Taylor had never been forward in approaching the opposite sex, not even in high school. She had always been quiet and kept to herself. The formation of relationships did not come easily for her since she always felt clumsy and awkward around guys. The fear of rejection and that of a possible negative outcome always managed to keep her at bay.

All her life she struggled with insecurities and fluctuating self-esteem. No matter what she accomplished or conquered, she was always left feeling as if she had to strive to be and do better than before or that of anyone else.

Jonathan was the complete opposite; he had absolutely no problem in the same areas. All of his life he had charm, character, popularity and endless counts of girls chasing after him. The only thing he longed for, yet couldn't obtain was the respect and approval of his father.

He desperately wanted his father to look upon him admiringly, with pride and respect; however, all his father ever did was focus on flaws or failures; no matter how big or small, placing all emphasis on the negative.

Throughout the time spent at college, Jonathan took absolutely no notice of Taylor whatsoever. He kept himself occupied with maintaining his popularity and hanging out with his exclusive group of friends. He had managed to obtain a notable reputation around campus for being a ladies man.

On weekends he never had to worry whether or not he would have a date; for the line was long with no end in sight of anxious females anticipating and competing to be near him, even if just for a short time. His allure was hypnotic and charisma effortless.

For all intended purposes, holding the title of "campus stud" was exhilarating and defining, but over time Jonathan began to realize his escapades and lifestyle was becoming more like work than play; along with the fact it was beginning to work against his life long goals and ambitions.

After some serious thought and consideration, it became apparent to him that he must make more suitable choices in his personal relationships; for he was now no longer a teenager and the antics that had once served him so well; now did anything but and at this stage in his life impressions mean everything.

With his newly acquired clarity and outlook; Jonathan took notice of Taylor for the first time, even though she had been around him all along. Instantly, he found himself captivated by her alluring beauty and poise. Everything about her intrigued him, from her statuesque form, bright smile, right down to her nervous quirks, such as twirling a strand of hair on her fingertip when she appeared to be nervous.

At first, he figured he would study her from afar in an attempt to learn all he could on his own, before mustering up the nerve to approach her. He couldn't explain it but for some unknown reason he had a sense that she was to be the one.

He knew she would be perfect in his life in so many ways, noting she was unlike the girls he had surrounded himself with for so many years; you could simply look at her and realize she was special, not dimwitted or shallow and by no means was she the type to be displayed as a trophy. Taylor was smart and sophisticated, a real class act.

Over the span of a few weeks, Jonathan passed up several opportunities to strike up a conversation with her, whether it was because he lost his nerve or just had a sense the timing wasn't right. Then it happened, on a particularly sunny and pleasant afternoon, he found himself approaching Taylor as she sat under a large shade tree on campus, reading a book.

With each antagonizing step, he could feel a strange sensation take hold, one he had never experienced; butterflies fluttering in his stomach along with a knot tugging in his throat, not to mention a pressing desire to flee in the opposite direction. Over the course of his life, never had he been so insecure or rattled by anyone, yet alone a girl; but somehow this was by far different from anything he had encountered before.

Each step bringing him closer to her, his nerves were testing him and his courage continually wavered by a small thread. While reading, Taylor noticed out of the corner of her eye the shadow of a figure coming towards her. Cautiously, she glanced to see if she could recognize the approaching form, amazed to discover the form belonged to Jonathan Reed.

She always remarked how she believed he could easily be a handsome movie star or even a male model; having all the necessary attributes, not lacking anywhere. On this day, he sported a pair of tan dress pants and a black button up dress shirt, with the top three buttons undone, giving off a sexy and relaxed appearance. She imagined he could likely wear just about anything and look like a million bucks, regardless if it were trendy or not.

As she admired him, he too was admiring her, finding her delicate features and soft complexion dramatically flawless. The spaghetti-strapped floral sundress she wore looked sweet and dazzling on her, complementing her lightly tanned skin. A soft, warm breeze gently dancing through the sky, filtered through her long hair just as he reached her at the tree.

For a brief moment, she wondered if she had fallen asleep, caught up in the midst of a dream and then began to wonder why Jonathan Reed would be standing before her, staring down at her. As soon as he spoke, she quickly cleared her mind; focused on every look, word, and detail in case she would need to replay the event over again in her head.

He smiled briskly before addressing her, as he asks, "Hello, may I join you?"

Taylor found it difficult to escape the amazement she was entangled within, nervously she replies, "Sure." Immediately, she began to feel overcome with fear and anxiety as he sat down directly across from her.

His eyes looking upon her warmly, he continues, "I'm Jonathan Reed."

She smiles before remarking, "Yes, I know. I've seen you around campus. We were actually in the same English class last semester. You sat two rows over from me. I'm Taylor Griffin."

As she held her hand out, Jonathan took her small hand in his, shaking it gently, feeling the soft contours of her hand and noticing how small it was inside of his own. It took a moment before he realized he had lost track of time and his mind had wandered off momentarily.

He felt his courage reappear after hearing she knew who he was and recounted where he sat in conjunction to her. This information provided a much needed ego boost. Unknowingly, a smile appeared on his face, revealing the superstar Taylor believed him to be.

With little thought or consideration, he quickly replies, "You're right, it slipped my mind." Immediately, he regretted the words he had just uttered, wishing he could take them back.

He continues, "I have actually wanted to talk to you before now, but I must confess; it has taken me awhile to conjure up enough nerve to approach you."

Taylor found herself surprised and somewhat flattered by the revelation; unable to imagine him fearful of anything or of anyone, as she professes, "I would never have guessed you to possess any of those qualities. You always seem so self-assured and outgoing, let alone to be nervous around someone like me."

He suddenly felt an urge to be forward and honest in place of boastful and condescending, remarking to her, "Yes, for the most part you're correct; however, for some unknown reason I can't explain, with you it is different. When I see you, I am overcome with butterflies and a feeling of nervousness I can't describe. I've never met anyone who had this type of effect on me."

This acknowledgement brought a warm smile to Taylor's face, yet she wondered if he was being sincere or if it was just a rehearsed play he performed for all the girls he chose to woo. Without question she wanted to believe the words he spoke, yet knowing his reputation and the type of girls he had always been seen with, she knew she didn't fit the mold.

Jonathan favored beautiful and shapely blondes; the types with perfect figures, real and fake tans, along with the trademark enhanced breasts; so why would he be interested in her? Could this possibly be some type of cruel prank? These thoughts raced around in her head.

Her eyes dropped to the ground as a smile crossed her face, stating, "I'm flattered. It isn't every day that I'm serenaded with compliments."

He looked at her with a look of disbelief, stating boastfully, "You're beautiful. I imagined you having guys lined up, hoping you'd honor them with your attention alone." His attempt at complimenting her came across more like a lame pick up line, in turn making his motives appear questionable.

Sensing his possible attempt of performing a cruel and heinous joke, she quickly looked to escape the introduction, replying in a matter of fact tone, "I'm sorry to disappoint you, but that isn't the case at all, nor has it ever been." She glanced down at her watch and stood up, continuing; "Jonathan, it was very nice talking with you. I hate to be the one to end our conversation, but I have a Calculus class to go to."

Without warning, he felt defeat take hold as he stood up and helped pick up her books, he asks, "Can I help you carry your books?"

She smiled, "No, thanks. I'm quite use to this. I appreciate the offer." Without any further indication, she began walking away.

Immediately, Jonathan sensed if he didn't make a lasting impression or effort, he would have no chance of redeeming himself, so without any further hesitation he asked, "Would you consider joining me for dinner?"

She looked back at him, quickly debating yes and no over in her head. She initially leaned towards no; however, for a reason she was uncertain of, she said yes instead. Immediately, Jonathan's face lit up, responding, "Great, how about this Friday? I know a great place in town."

His eagerness and delight outweighed his faulty approach, suddenly she found him to be a bit charming, "Friday night sounds great. I'll give you my number; you give me a call."

She jotted down her number on a small piece of pink paper and handed it to him, "I'm sorry Jonathan but I really must be going. Bye." As she rushed off to make her next class on time, Jonathan studied the small piece of paper and smiled at the realization he had passed the initial first step.

Later on that evening, at the girl's dorm, Taylor sat in the room she shared with her best friend Shannon Dupree, reading a book as she sat propped in the corner on her bed. She did her absolute best to focus on the book; however, her mind kept returning to Jonathan and their earlier encounter.

No matter how much she tried, she was unable to remove the smile from her face. Shannon entered the room, tossing her books on the floor and flopping down on her bed onto her back. Taylor's friend is tall, at least in comparison to her and in Taylor's opinion would have made an excellent basketball player had she been interested in sports.

Shannon's interests fell more in the category of style, fashion, and becoming a trendsetter. Her major was fashion and interior design. She excelled at both, yet her true love was designer clothing. Her light brown skin was always flawless, her bright smile warm and cheery, and her long black hair always styled to perfection.

Without taking notice of Taylor's joyful smile, she stared at the ceiling as if waiting for it to do a trick of some sort, in a tired voice, Shannon says, "Taylor, I cannot take much more of this!"

Taylor looked over at her friend trying not to break out in laughter, she remarks, "You do this at least once a week. Shannon, we are on the verge of graduating. You cannot get stressed out now."

Covering her face as she sat up, she continues, "I can't believe you can be so calm at a time like this, with our pending graduation in the midst and no guarantees that we'll pass; not to mention, the stress of exams and the looming reality of a future we are not prepared to embark upon."

Taylor smiled, cheerfully she says, "Speak for yourself. I can't wait to get out into the real world and put all that I've learned to work. I'm anxiously waiting to find the dream job that I've wanted ever since I was a young girl. Isn't the entire purpose of college to make your dreams a reality?"

Shannon looked at her friend, remarking with a positive lift in her voice, "You're right, I'm just being negative again. It will be fabulous! You will be a wonderful teacher and I will be a brilliant designer. My clothes will be worn by top models and celebrities. The glitz and glamour will shower me all around the world."

Taylor proudly boasts, "That's the spirit! We are going to make great things come our way, you'll see."

Taylor placed her book down, smiling at Shannon with excitement as though she could burst at any moment, "I met someone today," she announced.

Hearing those words, Shannon immediately became intrigued; asking, "Who is he?"

"I didn't mention it was a male," said Taylor.

Shannon shook her head from side to side as if to say no, "You didn't have to. Best friends can sense these things without hearing a word. Tell me all the juicy details."

Taylor began to tell the story with sheer delight, remarking, "Well, there isn't too much to tell as of yet. His name is Jonathan Reed; he came up to me in the courtyard today and asked me out. We have a date this Friday."

Shannon quickly interjects, "I believe I know who he is, correct me if I'm wrong, but isn't he the Casanova of the Campus?"

All of a sudden, Taylor felt as if she now had to defend him, "Yes, he has been linked with various girls, but he truly isn't what you'd expect."

Shannon moved over to Taylor's bed, sitting in front of her looking at her with a concerned expression, "Taylor, do you believe this guy to be sincere, even with his reputation?"

Her heart sank to know her friend didn't share the same enthusiasm as she herself did, yet knowing her mindset was in the same place earlier, she could understand her friend's concern.

Taylor replies, "I wouldn't agree to go out on a date with him if I didn't. Shannon, it is not as though I am rushing into anything. It is a date, not a walk down the aisle. If I discover he isn't the person I believe him to be, then I will break it off."

That night, Taylor laid in bed, thinking about Jonathan and as she drifted off to sleep she had a vision of her life in her not so distant future, a job as a teacher, a beautiful home in the suburbs, married to Jonathan, who is a successful lawyer, and two adoring children; a portrait of a wonderful life and family.

At the end of the week, the big night finally arrived. Jonathan picked Taylor up at her dorm, in his black BMW. He looked dashing in a pair of beige khaki pants with a light blue button up dress shirt. The shirt formed to his body perfectly, outlining the contours of his muscular frame. He flashed one of his famous smiles at her as she walked towards him.

As Taylor was admiring how stunning he looked as she got closer to him, he found himself in awe over just how breathtaking she was, in a sheer black blouse that hung loosely at the edges of her shoulders with a black skirt resting just above the knees. A warm and gentle breeze raced through her hair; creating a magical illusion the closer she got to him.

He noticed one side of her blouse had slipped off her shoulder, revealing the strap of a silk under top. As she casually slid it back in place, he began to feel a driving urge to gently caress her neck and shoulder, trying diligently to forget the sight of her bare skin.

To him, Taylor embodied all that he could and would ever want in a spouse; intellect, ambition, spirit, beauty and sensitivity. Just in being near her, he found himself feeling more alive and awakened than he ever had; he only hoped she felt the same or could, over the course of time.

Throughout their first date, Jonathan remained a perfect gentleman; opening the car door and allowing her to walk ahead of him. At first, all the common awkwardness and unfamiliarity dominated the situation as both found it difficult to warm up to the other.

As they sat at the table, waiting for their dinner, Jonathan took it upon himself to break the ice, "You look very beautiful. I'm having difficulty in looking away, so please forgive me if I appear to stare."

Taylor smiled, "Thank you. You look very handsome."

She glanced around the restaurant, admiring its quaint simplicity and charm.

Plants hung throughout, giving it a wild jungle like atmosphere. Small candles lit up each small circular table. The dim lighting shadowed the surrounding couples, while illuminating each individual table as though a small spotlight shone on each one.

"This is a lovely restaurant. I've never been here before" she remarked.

He looked around the room briskly and then reconnected his eyes with hers, "It is a great place. I know the owner, Gino. He's a great guy. I've grown accustomed to this place over the past few years. It is far more grown up than most college hangouts."

Without any warning, Taylor began to feel a rush of anxiety come over her, she started to fidget with her hands as they rested on her lap, wishing the ease would take hold and the horrible terror of feeling at a loss for words would simply subside.

Jonathan sensed her discomfort; he inquires "What is your major?"

She smiled; relieved that he spoke up first, she says "I'm obtaining a teaching degree. I want to be an elementary school teacher. I've dreamt of doing so ever since I was a little girl. My mother is a teacher; I've always idolized her and aspired to be just like her. There are many private schools in New York. I've already begun applying to several of them."

He looked at her warmly, "That is a noble profession. Not an easy one either. I don't think I could handle the stress and pressure of being in charge of a room full of small children."

Jonathan grinned as Taylor responds to his comment with a smile, "I'm sure you would do just fine at entertaining kids. You'd probably surprise yourself. It just takes patience and a warm heart."

"I think it is great that you have insight on transitioning from college to a career. I need to be as focused as you are. It isn't much longer until graduation. Time has a way of passing so rapidly, whether you're prepared or not," remarks Jonathan.

The mood and atmosphere became relaxed, allowing Taylor to feel more at ease. "Jonathan, where do you intend to practice law?"

"I'm from Chicago, all of my family and friends are there; however, I doubt I'll go back. New York is the place to build a career in the large scale law firms and I have no reservations that I won't find what I'm looking for in a career," states Jonathan.

His warm brown eyes looked upon her softly as he continues, "I've worked diligently over all my years in school and I intend to see that it pays off. I believe you have to find what it is you want in life and grab for it with both hands. You can't wait and hope for it to make its way to you."

Taylor had a profound sense that Jonathan hadn't just described his pending career, but also his passion for everything he sought after. She curiously wondered if she could possibly be in his sights as well.

CHAPTER 2

A BRILLANT DISGUISE

A s thoughts of the past continue to replay in her head; the phone rings, startling her back into the present. She answers the phone, still a little rattled, she says, "Hello."

Jonathan's voice sounds from the other end, "Taylor, I'm sorry honey, but I'm going to be working late again tonight. I'll be home as soon as I can, I promise."

She replies without pause, "I'll wait up for you."

Jonathan quickly responds with a short tone in his voice, "No...I mean there is no reason for you to wait up. I don't know how long I will be here and there isn't any sense in you staying up waiting for me. I have to go. I love you. Bye." He hangs up, ending the call before she has an opportunity to utter another word.

Surprisingly, after eleven years together; Jonathan still has himself convinced that his wife is none the wiser and believes every lie to exit his mouth. It was two years earlier when Taylor became suspicious and stumbled across his indiscretions.

One occasion validated the lingering clues for her, when she prepared dinner in a picnic basket with her special linguini, bread, and wine to take to his office to surprise him with a late dinner, while he worked over; only to discover he wasn't at work and had actually left early, as a bookkeeper had unknowingly informed her.

She had returned home, dining on the food alone and waiting for him to return. At around 2 AM he came tiptoeing into the apartment, surprised to see his wife sitting on the sofa waiting for him.

He gave her the now usual spiel and apology, stating "I'm sorry, honey. I have a huge caseload right now. If I want to make partner, I have to be willing to put in the long hours."

Many, many times she thought of confronting him and letting him know she knew his secrets and lies, but found herself letting it go, up to the point that she no longer troubled herself to even think about it.

Her life had spiraled out of control in so many ways. She found she lost all knowledge of who she was or the person she had now become.

It wasn't that she was comfortable or secure in the knowledge that her husband now chose to be unfaithful to her, it was just a fact she had come to accept. The thought of leaving him entered her mind several times, yet strangely enough she wasn't ready to walk out on her marriage. Even if it meant less to him, it still held value for her.

Across town, in a luxurious penthouse suite, Jonathan looks at his reflection in a mirror, studying himself as if attempting to understand the reflection, who looks like him yet, is not the person he remembers.

His hair still similarly thick and full as in his college days: while maintaining a presentable look for the courtroom and sustaining an appearance of wildness. A few noticeable wrinkles around the eyes begin to show his age, and his neatly trimmed short-length beard and mustache add character and sex appeal.

His focus is disrupted when Karla Ferguson, a stunningly beautiful blonde who is twenty-five years old; walks up behind him pressing her naked body against his back and wrapping her arms around his muscular chest. Her petite figure and surgically enhanced breasts make it difficult to overlook her, even when in the middle of a crowded room.

She gazes in the mirror at his reflection; asking, "Do you feel badly for lying to your wife again in order to be here with me?"

He looks away from his reflection, attempting to escape the guilt that begins to rise up from within, "Of course I don't feel good about lying to my wife. I go through this in my mind over and over again. I have absolutely no reason to be cheating on my wife and yet I continue to do so, with you."

As he turns to face Karla, she gently caresses the left side of his face, gazing into his troubled eyes, stating, "Jon, I've told you before, if you wish to break off what we have, that's fine. I can't say I wouldn't miss our times together, but I'll understand your reasons for doing so. Just say the word."

A mischievous smile appears on his face as he lifts her off the floor, "You make it far too easy to want to stay. As long as she doesn't know I'm not working and continues to believe in all of my late nights, I don't foresee any reason why this has to end. I love my wife, but there are things she doesn't offer me in our marriage that I have with you," remarks Jonathan.

Back on the ground, Karla begins to laugh, as she states "I don't believe that she doesn't offer you what you want but more so that I offer you all that is carefree and dangerous. The thrill by far means more to you than anything else. You forget how well I've come to know you over the past two years."

Gazing at his mistress's naked body, he replies, "You're right, you may in fact know me better than I know myself." As with most visits, the two remain behind closed doors, having passionate sex until it becomes evident that he must return home to his wife.

―――――

At the same time, Taylor enjoys a love affair of her own while Jonathan is away, an icy and smooth character of rum and Coke. Unbeknownst to her the attraction has developed into a common habit. It offers nothing more than a deterrent from the anger and resentment she feels for the impropriety of her husband.

With her glass in hand, she makes her way through the large dimly lit apartment to the office where Jonathan spends most of his time when he is on occasion at home. She sits in his large, leather desk chair, taking large gulps from her drink, while gazing at their wedding picture on top of his desk, which seems to stare at her with daunting eyes. The photo reflects a time so different, when together they were so happy and in love.

They had continued to date steadily throughout the remainder of college and after graduating, Jonathan had asked Taylor to move in with him. He had expressed to her right away that he could not fathom moving on with his life unless she was a part of it.

She fell quick and hard for his good looks, charm and sweet promises. Everything seemed so perfect and as if all was going to go as planned. Taylor had found the man of her dreams and delighted in the idea of starting a life together. Jonathan was driven with ambition and the desire to discover his own success and riches, with a beautiful wife by his side.

He had the ability to make Taylor so very happy; spoiling her constantly with gifts, large and small. Trinkets of breathtaking jewelry: stunning large bouquets of flowers, and an expensive sports car; which he ended up driving most of the time.

Once a year, he would surprise her with a vacation to an exotic place, just as with the first, when after graduation he swept her off to the Bahamas for two weeks. It was a dream-like paradise; lying around on the warm sand in the hot sun, starlit walks hand in hand along the beach, romantic dinners just the two of them in their suite.

Passionate evenings spent making love until dawn, huddled together watching as the sun would rise over the ocean. They didn't want to see an end come to their tropical getaway, but as with all treasured things, it had to end sooner or later.

A new life awaited both of them back in New York. Jonathan had landed a position at the prestigious law firm of Tyler, Franklin, Calhoun and Calhoun: one of the oldest and prestigious firms in New York, representing high-powered clients near and abroad.

He was so excited at landing his dream job; Taylor, however, hadn't been as fortunate in making her dreams materialize. She had pursued her job search with just as much dedication and vigor as Jonathan had, yet found herself being rejected at each and every attempt. Throughout, Jonathan remained supportive and encouraging with each rejection letter; telling her not to worry for the right job would present itself when the time was right.

In his attempt to make her feel needed and her role as the love of his life, he often remarked how much he found comfort in her being at home and able to attend various functions to aid him in his climb to the top.

For Taylor, she wanted to be supportive and back him in every aspect, yet not having a career of her own did not appeal to her. She felt a loss of identity and a lack of self-worth. All the hard work and dedication of furthering her education and here she was, standing on the sidelines while witnessing his soaring career. She did her best not to allow herself to be jealous or bitter, but at times it often won out.

As Taylor continued applying for various job openings as the months continued to pass, Jonathan took her out for a romantic dinner to lift her spirits. His spirits were elated and happier than she had ever seen him before. He chose an expensive restaurant, Rivera, to celebrate a special occasion; however, he wouldn't reveal any other details. Knowing it wasn't the mark of any type of anniversary, she anxiously awaited the big news.

They embodied such exuberance together, a stunning couple; both dressed with style and elegance. Taylor wore a luring red silk dress with an open back and a matching long trailing scarf around her neckline. Jonathan displayed flair in a stylish and expensive Armani suit, which looked as if it was personally tailored to fit him alone.

The two walked through the restaurant hand in hand, receiving glances from other couples that happened to find themselves drawn to study their entrance. The depth of their love and affection for one another was so intriguing and obvious as they walked arm in arm.

Seated in a private corner, Jonathan ordered a bottle of their finest champagne. Taylor patiently waited for him to clue her in; all the while he purposely withheld any details, knowing it was driving her mad.

Moments later, only managing to get a few chuckles and smiles from him, she could take no more suspense; she says "Jonathan, when are you going to let me in on this special occasion?"

He smiled affectionately, cleverly remarking "You can't stand it any longer, can you? My dear, this is going to be a night to remember for the rest of our lives."

Desperately she wanted to guess where he was heading with this, yet she knew she was ill-equipped, she asks "How long are you planning on keeping this a secret?"

He reached across the table, taking her hand, softly remarking "We must have the champagne first. This has to be done right."

Both held their champagne glasses, preparing to make a toast, Jonathan begins, "I have been given the best news. I was offered one of the most important cases of the year. I will be representing Stephen Rogers, the CEO of Continental Enterprises. This is my shot to prove myself and move up the corporate ladder."

Taylor smiled all the while feeling as though this is just another slap in the face for her; another successful victory for Jonathan, while her life hung in the balance. Quickly, she told herself not to be so insensitive and self-involved; after all he had worked very hard and put a great deal into getting to where he is now.

Looking at him admiringly, she replies, "Congratulations! I am thrilled for you. This is such an important milestone. It is about time all of your hard work, dedication, and long hours paid off."

He completed his toast by tapping his glass with Taylor's, "Baby, this is for both of us. You have stood by me through every step of this amazing journey. I would not be the man I am today if it wasn't for you."

She smiled softly as she remarks, "Jonathan, I am so very proud of you. This is the greatest news."

He looked at her with a sparkle in his eyes and grinned slightly, he states "It may turn out to not be the greatest news after all, but that will greatly depend on you." She looked at him with a quizzical expression as she noticed him removing a small black velvet box, sliding it across the table in front of her.

Glancing from the small box back to Jonathan, she could feel her heart skip a beat. As though he was unable to take the suspense himself, he tells her, "Go ahead and open it."

Carefully, she lifted the small box open as steadily as her shaking hands were capable of, quickly having her breath taken away by the dazzling five-carat diamond ring gazing up at her.

Tears began to well up in her eyes, "Jonathan, this is the most beautiful thing I've ever seen."

He got down on one knee, taking her hand in his as he looked lovingly into her eyes, asking, "Taylor Marie Griffin, will you marry me?"

She let out a short giggle, "Jonathan, I would be honored to be your wife. Yes, I will marry you." She bent down closer to him, holding his face within her hands, kissing him passionately.

With pure pride, he slipped the ring on her finger, "You have made this the greatest night of my life, making all of my dreams come true. This is a night we will never forget."

━━━◆━━━

Pulling herself back to the present, she rises from the desk and returns to the kitchen to refresh her drink, before making her way to the bedroom. The person she longed to become is just a memory; her life, now consists of being a lawyer's wife, a life sized trophy wife that her husband parades around at parties and functions, as if she were a first place prize he won in a contest.

Awhile back, things appeared to show some promise. Taylor was offered a teaching position. It wasn't the exact position she was looking for, but at least it was work and in the field she wanted to be a part of: The Rivermont Elementary School located ten miles from the apartment, teaching 5th graders. The principal was so impressed by her resume and felt she would be a refreshing change in a much lacking willingness to learn atmosphere, which currently existed within the school.

She was thrilled at the job offer and when Principal Ralph Jones told her she could take a few days to think it over; she jumped at the opportunity and accepted the position on the spot. All day, she remained on cloud nine, arriving home in a chipper mood and browsing her wardrobe to find the perfect outfit to wear on her first day.

Jonathan noticed her transformation right away, "What's going on?" he asked curiously.

Running over, hugging him tightly, "The greatest thing has finally happened. I'm still in shock. One of the teaching positions I applied for a few weeks ago, they called me in today for an interview. It is the Rivermont Elementary School. It is a ten mile drive, but that won't be much of an issue. Anyway, the principal of the school; Ralph Jones, he was so impressed with my resume; he offered me the job right on the spot! Isn't it wonderful?"

He smiled momentarily and then lost the smile as a negative expression took hold, he asks, "Taylor, why didn't you call me and let me know you had an interview?"

A bit confused by his sudden demeanor, she responds, "Well, with having so many rejections, I didn't want to make something out of it unless it actually turned into a possibility. I'm sorry for not calling you beforehand, but look how wonderful this is; I now have a job too."

She watched him closely to witness his eyes taking on a look so angry and volatile, as he asks, "Wait, how do you figure you have the job, because it was offered to you?!"

A sense of fear began to take hold of her, "No, Jonathan, because I accepted it. I begin on Monday. I thought you'd be happy for me. This will get me out of the apartment and allow me to be a teacher, which I've wanted all along."

He sat on the sofa, appearing as if the news he had just heard was positively earth shattering. Looking up at her, he softly remarks, "Baby, I'm sorry, I realize this is a life long dream for you and I'm not trying to put a damper on it, but I just wish you had mentioned this to me before accepting the position."

Jonathan continues, "Now is not a good time for any changes or transitions. The firm has an opening on the board and I'm a promising candidate. This could very well lead to an opportunity to my becoming a partner. I need for you to be by my side while I move up within the company. Once I'm a partner, you can pursue your teaching career. Right now just isn't the right time."

Tears began to stream down her face, as she asks, "You're telling me I can't take the job?"

He stood up, looking sympathetically into her eyes, "No, baby, not right now, please understand, I don't want to hold you back, but when the partners pay huge attention to what your home life consists of, it is important that we remain a model couple. I'm asking you to sacrifice a lot and for that I'm truly sorry. Please try to understand that by doing this you are aiding me in sealing our future."

He smiled at her, "I know you don't want to live in this apartment forever, just as I don't and right around the corner is my promotion, a house in the suburbs, children, and your teaching career," says Jonathan.

CHAPTER 3

AN EVIL FROM WITHIN

N OW, TWELVE years since they first met her marriage now consisted of domination and control. Initially, every aspect was wonderful, magical, and beyond what she could have ever imagined possible. Suddenly and without warning, it had all begun to unravel.

To see her marriage deteriorating, saddened her immensely, yet she had no idea how to fix it; if it was in fact able to be mended. Anytime she brought up counseling or therapy, Jonathan would give her a look as if to say she was crazy and without merit to suggest such an action. He was convinced there was no problem and stuck to the assumption this was just an attempt on her part to obtain attention.

Leaving him was never considered as an option. She did; however, have many regrets and knew if she had it to do all over again; she would certainly do things a lot differently. Without question, she often wished she had never met Jonathan Reed.

At around 3 AM; Jonathan enters the apartment quietly. Looking as if he had just stepped out of bed; his hair in disarray, clothes wrinkled, and his dress shirt improperly buttoned. Carefully placing his briefcase down on top of a small table near the door then proceeding through the apartment.

A small light shines across the apartment, from the master bedroom. As he makes his way into the room, he finds his wife asleep in bed clutching onto a teddy bear he bought her for Valentine's Day two years earlier. She looks content and peaceful as she sleeps.

He covers her up and picks up the empty glass on the nightstand, smelling the inside for a distinction of its former contents. A vague scent of rum lingers in the glass. Too often he has come home to find his wife in the same state. With a focus and steady concentration, he undresses and climbs into bed, purposely facing away from Taylor. No longer does he cuddle against her or hold her close.

The next morning, Taylor wakes in bed just as she fell asleep, alone. She slips on her robe, attempts to regain her bearings and makes her way through the apartment in search of Jonathan. The lingering after effects of the alcohol still has a hold on her.

Not hearing any sounds or motion, she assumes he has already left for work, but as she enters the kitchen she is surprised to see him sitting at the small dinette table eating a bagel and having his morning coffee. She does her best to cover up her hangover, smiling, she states, "Good morning. Why didn't you wake me? I could have fixed you a real breakfast."

Jonathan looks at her with a disapproving glance, "Taylor, I honestly don't believe much could have woken you up. How many times do I have to tell you I do not want you drinking? We have been over this too many times to count. If you continue to do as I ask you not to; I'll treat you like a child. I will remove the alcohol entirely if need be. If you persist, I will take even further drastic measures."

Often he came across as a father figure, telling her what to wear, what to order, what to drink, when she could go somewhere and punish her when he felt it was appropriate. He was no longer a loving husband, but more like a warden and their home like a prison.

Too many times she has heard this speech. The anger and hostility suddenly begins to rise inside and before she knows it the words just slide right off her tongue, "Jonathan, I'm not drunk. I do not drink all the time. I had two glasses last night and that was all. I do not understand why you insist upon making more out of this than it is."

Standing up with his coffee cup in hand, Jonathan says, "You don't seem to fathom that you have a problem. This affects me. I do not need the label of the attorney with the drunken wife."

The statement infuriates her, responding angrily, "This is your utmost priority, your job comes first and that is what you're most concerned with. It is though you married your job, not me."

Standing three feet from her, his eyes blazing with pure evil; he walks slowly towards her, "Don't become cross with me. I won't have it. Yes, my job is important. You are also very important to me. I wouldn't have married you if you weren't. You have to think about things before doing them. In part, I know it's my fault for you feeling lonely and down. I'll do my best to get home earlier when I'm able. Please lay off the drinking."

She feels a sense of shame for acting out, hugging him she begins to wonder if now wouldn't be a good time to address getting a job, looking up into his eyes, "Jonathan, please let me apply for a teaching job. I need to get out of this apartment and do something with my life. By me finding work, it will prove to be an asset to your placement in the firm, not hinder you. I promise."

He pulls away from her, "We have been through this, Taylor, this is not the time."

This time, she doesn't contemplate a response she just unleashes it, "There will never be a right time. You do not want me to work. Your entire intention is to keep a close watch over me, as I remain your captive within this cell of an apartment, to be at your beck and call. That isn't fair to me. This is not the life I wanted for myself."

Without warning, Jonathan's face tenses up; his eyes become angrily fixated on Taylor and then with a sudden move, he strikes her across the face, knocking her to the floor, with a harsh tone he says, "You are so ungrateful! I have made a lavish and well-to-do lifestyle for the both of us, working day and night, and this is the thanks I get in return. You have nerve to get self-righteous with me!"

She struggles on the floor to hold herself up, fearful to look at him, yet uncertain of any possible backlash; she listens closely as he walks out of the room, leaving her on the floor. She begins to cry as she pulls herself upright, gripping onto one of the barstools near the counter. Shock and confusion best describe her state of mind.

A sharp, nagging pain throbs within her jaw. As she stands up and releases her grip from the barstool, attempting to balance herself, she feels her life spiraling out of control. In all of their years together, he had never struck her or even raised his hand to her, until now. There had been many heated arguments followed by short stinted silent treatments, but nothing of this malice and cruelty.

She carefully makes her way to the bathroom, locking the door behind her. With the first glance at her reflection in the mirror, she is horrified. Quivering with fear, she looks at her left cheek and the distinctive red mark where his hand struck her face. Attempting to be brave, she does her best not to cry and just focus on tending to her battered face with a damp washcloth.

Each touch sends a jolt of pain through her face. Thoughts begin to race in her head, wondering how it could have come down to this. Jonathan was no longer the man she fell in love with, nor was he the person she wanted to be with any longer. Her marriage was a sham and the heartache of years of disappointment had taken their toll.

Deep down, she knew this had to end. She would have to weigh the pros and cons of her marriage and make a fateful decision. If he no longer loved her, then he too needed to move on. A marriage cannot survive the constant anger, resentment, hostility and deception. She wanted what they had in the past and she was convinced she could not continue with a future consisting of the present.

Suddenly, the doorknob of the locked bathroom door turns. Taylor jumps back as her heart plummets. A soft, loving voice sounds from the other side, as Jonathan pleads, "Taylor, please come out. I want to apologize." She hesitates as she focuses intently on the doorknob, not sure she wants to be face to face with him or if she's ready to trust him quite yet.

Cautiously, she opens the door. He looks at her sympathetically and smiles, "Baby, I'm sorry. I wasn't thinking clearly. I let my emotions get the better of me. I have never hit you before and I can't believe I just did. I am so sorry. I promise you, I will never hurt you in any way, ever again. Please forgive me," states Jonathan. As he reaches a hand towards her face, she quickly pulls away, "I promise," he continues. He touches her face gently, kissing her softly on the lips.

As he kisses her, she finds she is nauseated and angered by his manner. Inside, she feels various emotions ready to erupt within like a volcano, releasing her own steam and volatile contents.

A short time later, Jonathan comes out of the master bedroom, ready for work. As he stands at a distance, watching Taylor as she sits quietly in an oversized chair with her legs resting on the matching ottoman, gazing out at the morning sky as it makes its crest over the towering buildings; he notices how unhappy she appears.

He dislikes seeing her this way and knows he happens to be partially to blame. For all of his flaws and bad judgments, he was still very much in love with his wife and it physically pained him to see her miserable and unpleased in their marriage. He knew he would have to do something to turn this around.

While he was in the shower, he thought long and hard on what he had done. He knew striking her was the wrong thing to do, no matter how much she angered or provoked him. Lashing out with violent rage was not the answer.

He had never struck her before and without question he wasn't proud of himself for doing so, it actually made him feel like a coward.

He couldn't explain how the rage took control of him, causing him to react so violently.

When he was younger, he had never retained any type of violent behavior; this sudden occurrence seemed to give him a completely different personality, one that had been so unfamiliar to him.

In pinpointing precisely when their marriage began to falter or his desire to become unfaithful came about, he could not say. Taylor had always been such a warm and loving wife as she continued to be as each year came to pass. At times, he wished she wasn't so perfect just to aid him in the ability to look at his own reflection in the mirror each day.

Jonathan knew just how lucky he was to have her in his life. To lose her was not something he would ever allow to happen, no matter what. His identity was intertwined with his relationship with Taylor, to be without her, he would be nothing and all that he had worked so hard to become and obtain would be lost forever. She had always been and would always be his everything.

Cautiously and with a precision stride, he makes his way across the room towards his wife's side, bending down kissing her undamaged cheek as he feels dire need to repent for his misdeeds, he whispers to her, "I have to go to work. I'll make it up to you this evening, I promise. I love you very much, do you know that?"

In a quiet and quivering voice, she replies, "Yes. I love you too."

Once the apartment is her own, she stands in the shower, posed in a fixed position, leaning against the aqua blue ceramic tiles of the exquisite full length glass shower. As the hot water drenches her body, she finds she can't stop thinking about the drastic change of events within her marriage.

She grapples with the question how she could not have seen this coming and what exactly led to such an enormous backlash. Could she truthfully be unappreciative; for she knew he did wonderful things to make her happy.

Having a failed marriage was not supposed to happen. Even with her loving him with all she is, she knows she cannot survive a marriage of deception or domestic violence. She had compromised a lot over the course of their marriage but one area she would stand firm would be her integrity and self-strength. If things are to improve it will have to be a team effort.

Arriving to work, Jonathan stops briskly at his secretary's desk appearing to be contemplating an idea, he says "Jill, I need for you to have a dozen long stem red roses sent to my wife at home. Actually, order two other varied arrangements as well. She isn't feeling well and I think it will make her feel a little bit better." He smiles and continues, "Also, I need for you to make airplane reservations for Australia for next week."

Jill smiles curiously, asking "Are you and Mrs. Reed planning a well deserved vacation to the beach house?"

"Yes, I think it is a great idea. After all, we own the house in Queensland and it has been awhile since we were last there. This time of year, it will be lovely there. Taylor loves the beach and the shops. I have a number of client contacts I need to touch base with there," remarks Jonathan.

Shaking her head from side to side in approval, she says, "Look at you, always thinking about work. You know that's the reason to take a vacation; to get away from work and anything work related, so you can focus on more important things, like relaxing, rekindling the romance, or even contemplating the start of a family."

Jonathan gives a subtle smile as he replies, "You're right. It has been too long. Let me know when you have the tickets. I want to surprise Taylor this evening."

Later that morning, Taylor stands in front of the full length mirror in her bedroom, wearing jeans, a dark brown oversized sweater, dark brown clogs and a crocheted brown cap. She arranges a pair of sunglasses and tugs on the sides of the small snug cap, pressing her hair against her cheeks.

Once she feels confident that she has concealed the bruise on her cheek, she grabs her full length suede coat and heads out the front door to go visit her college chum, who just happens to be back in town for a short stay.

Although the two rarely see one another due to Shannon's hectic work schedule, they always keep in touch and see each other when time permits. Unlike Taylor, Shannon did follow through with her dreams and ambitions. She breezed onto the fashion scene and over the course of several years managed to come into her own. She started her own clothing line and at first had a small consumer based market, which over time grew into a global market.

Shannon made her best attempts to include Taylor and make her feel as if she was a part of her success, often offering to make her a partner, a silent one if necessary, if she felt Jonathan would oppose. She despised the way Jonathan sidelined any of her attempts to work and her efforts to be independent from him.

There would periodically be times when Shannon would make no efforts to hold back, telling Taylor exactly what she thought of him, yet Taylor always stood by Jonathan and explained that she just didn't know the loving and caring side of him as she did.

Taylor arrives at the large brick, factory sized studio apartment her friend had purchased and completely remodeled. She had one side made into a lavish apartment and the other section was her studio. Taking a deep breath; hesitating at first to knock, she holds her fist up and then forces herself to knock.

Shannon beams with joy at the sight of her friend, and then loses it all once she catches a glimpse of the bruise on her cheek, Shannon asks, "Did Jonathan hit you?"

Taylor immediately pulls at her hair attempting to pull it over her cheek, "He did and he apologized for it. We were arguing and I provoked him."

Shannon quickly interjects, "Oh, no you don't! Don't dare try to defend him for this, what is wrong with you? You are a very smart girl; you know this isn't a good thing. Once it begins it will never end. You need to leave him. I don't know why you've stayed this long. You discovered his indiscretions, knowing odds are he's still seeing someone behind your back; he refuses to let you get a job, and now this! You need to just cut your losses and move on."

Having heard this speech before, she attempts to do her best to just brush it off, "I appreciate your concern and I know you have my best interest at heart, but this will work itself out. I'm not defending what he did and his apology does not get him off the hook. I love him and I know we are all capable of actions that occur on impulse, which we end up regretting," says Taylor.

Shannon looks at her friend sympathetically, "He has done this to you once and therefore in all likelihood, he'll do it again. He may even acquire a taste for it. I've never cared for his temper or rash demeanor."

Quickly, Taylor aims to change the subject, she says, "I want to hear all about Paris, every little detail. Tell me everything!"

As the afternoon draws closer, the two sit and talk over Shannon's adventures in the fashion world; sitting in the quaint and stylish living room, with white leather furniture and sheer pink drapes, with matching pillows throughout the room.

Taylor smiles with pride, "I am so happy for you. One day, in the near future, I will join you on one of your trips to a foreign land," Taylor boasts cheerfully.

A glimmer of hope lights up in Shannon's eyes, as she states, "Oh, I do hope so. Traveling with the companionship of my best friend would make it all the more enjoyable. I can't fathom Jonathan agreeing to the idea. He must have you at his beck and call. I would suggest he accompany you, but odds are he wouldn't agree to that either."

Taylor glances down as if considering her reply, she says, "You never know, he could always surprise you. Don't immediately count this out. Besides, I've taken a number of trips back home, without him mind you and it went splendidly well."

Deep down, Taylor knows what her friend says is the truth, for Jonathan has always been leery and cautious of any man that dared to utter a word or glance her way. On one occasion, while at the movies, he caught a stranger glancing at his wife more than once, and after the film was over he followed him out of the theatre and proceeded to rough him up as Taylor watched and pleaded with him to stop.

Taylor reassures her friend, "Jonathan is not fearful of me meeting someone else. He knows he has absolutely nothing to worry about. I just have to be close by for now while he's working his way up within the firm."

Shannon looks at her with disbelief, "I can't understand how you've actually convinced yourself that this entire idea is truth. He tells you that over and over to hold you off on traveling and having a career of your own and then once he has accomplished one thing or another, then he comes up with something new. It is a vicious, never-ending cycle and one in which you will never break. I hate seeing him treat you this way," says Shannon.

She begins to feel as if her friend is using her as a punching bag in order to make her feel horrible about herself, which she happens to have succeeded at. Taylor says, "You're right; I put my life on hold so he can advance his own. I don't like sitting on the sidelines, watching as everyone else follows their dreams, while I'm still waiting to make mine materialize, but for now, this is something I must endure until I can make things happen for me. I haven't given up on what I want, believe me."

Shannon looks at her friend with caring eyes, as she asks, "When will that be, Taylor? You're thirty-three years old. Time isn't going to just stand still while you wait for a window of opportunity."

With a smile, lightening the conversation, as Taylor jokingly says, "Thanks a lot. That means so much coming from you. Could you be a little harsher in the failure of my life next time?"

Shannon giggles, "Hey, I didn't mean for it to be hurtful, just truthful. You cannot continue to give into him. Stand up for yourself and your part in this marriage. If he has his way, you will remain a trophy wife; with nothing but him and then what will you do if he ever decides to leave you for someone else?"

As if a sudden bolt of lightening jolted her right in the place she sat, she began to contemplate her friend had a valid point. Jonathan had an excellent job, apartment, cars, while she had no job or real assets of her own.

Shannon hugs Taylor, "Don't be fearful of losing what you have. If you were meant to have it then it will remain, if it leaves; then it wasn't meant to stay. I know it sounds difficult, but you have to change the things you can and let the rest fall as it may. You should never be fearful of making positive changes," states Shannon.

CHAPTER 4

TWO TICKETS TO PARADISE

T AYLOR RETURNS home from visiting her friend Shannon at around 4 PM. As she places her belongings on the small console table inside the entrance of the living room, she notices the red light on the answering machine blinking, as if signally an urgent alarm.

She stands momentarily staring at the blinking light, knowing whom the message belongs to without doubt or question. Suddenly she finds herself trembling with fear and anxiety. With all her might and intuition, she'd love nothing more than to delete the message without listening to it, yet she knows she has to play it.

Pressing the play button, the message begins, "Taylor, it is 10:00. I was calling to see how you're feeling. Call me as soon as you get this message. I love you," says Jonathan. With her hand resting on top of the receiver, she debates whether or not to call him back now or later and then decides there is no point in delaying the inevitable.

Jonathan's secretary, Jill, answers the phone, "Jonathan Reed's office, Jill speaking, may I help you?"

"Hi, Jill, this is Taylor. Is Jonathan available?"

"Mrs. Reed, one moment I'll check for you." Taylor hangs on the line, hoping he is in one of his usual meetings.

Without any warning or warm greeting, Jonathan begins "Where have you been?"

Calmly she replies, "I went to visit Shannon. She's in town and getting ready to leave for Paris. She won't be back for several months."

His voice softens, "I wanted to apologize to you again for my inappropriate behavior this morning. How are you feeling?"

Taylor begins thumbing through a catalog resting near the phone, half way focusing on the conversation wishing it would end, "I'm fine. There's a bruise on my cheek, but I'm sure it will disappear in a day or so."

He lets out an exasperated sigh as he replies, "Taylor, why would you go visit your friend with a bruise on your face? What were you thinking? You had to know it would be noticed and remarked upon. I don't want people thinking I beat you up, which is clearly not the case. Did she ask you what happened?"

This line of questioning angered her more than anything else. It was clear he was more concerned about how others would perceive him, little else mattered. "Yes, but that was the extent of it. I explained it was an accident," remarks Taylor.

With the tone of his voice altering, she could easily sense his resentment and hostility, "Taylor, I don't need this or any bad publicity. You just don't think some times."

In that moment, she is convinced she cannot love such a man, one who is considerate of only his own feelings and persona. His inconsiderate and demeaning words cause the anger and resentment to rage from within, she says, "Jonathan, she would never do that to me or even to you."

Jonathan pauses for a moment, "Taylor, I just want you to use better judgment in the future. I have to go. I'll be home this evening around 6:30, I promise. There is a great deal of work I have to get done before then. I'll see you later. I love you."

Before preparing dinner, Taylor takes a hot bubble bath with numerous candles lit in the room. She further sets the tone with some relaxing music playing from the built in wall unit. In no time, she is relaxed and at ease thinking of visiting far away, exotic places.

She becomes lost within her tranquil and happy setting; regretting having to return to reality in time to prepare dinner. Time forces her to get out and struggle through the confusing task of selecting something to wear for dinner. Searching through her entire closet, she can't decide on what to wear.

Pondering whether she should dress subtle, casual, romantic, or sexy. By all accounts she isn't in the mood to go for romantic or sexy, she would be simply contented to be casual and comfortable. With all due respect, the events of the day didn't quite do the trick in aiding her in feeling attractive.

At last, she comes across a dress she bought for a cocktail party that ended up being cancelled, which she hadn't actually worn; a stylish and sexy little black Versace number.

She studies her reflection in the full length mirror, finding the dress compliments her slender figure and shows off her toned legs. Her figure is close to perfection, not too muscular but toned enough to have the right amount of muscle definition.

One plus with being at home all day, she had the time to focus and care for herself, exercising on a daily basis. Not to say she was a health conscience person, because anyone who knew Taylor knew just how much she loved chocolate and other sweets.

Her skin still very youthful with just a little hint of her true age allowed her to often be mistaken for someone who is twenty-five years old, which always flattered her.

All of the married couples her age had moved on to the next big stage in their lives, buying a house, having children and making investments for retirement and college. Taylor wanted the same, yet she felt she would never get past the early stages of marriage, even though she no longer was in the classification of a newly wed.

Twenty minutes later, Jonathan arrives home, exactly at the time he promised he would. He immediately takes notice of the candlelit apartment, smiling at the magnificent table display, styled with perfection as if placed in the middle of a five star restaurant.

He peers around the room to see if he can catch a glimpse of Taylor. As he places his briefcase and jacket on the chair near the living room, he notices her walking into the dim light in the living room. His breath is taken away at the sight of his stunning wife, dressed elegantly yet very sexy.

She walks up to him, with a warm and sultry look in her eyes, she begins to loosen his tie; "Dinner is just about ready. I can keep it warm if you'd like to take a shower first," says Taylor.

He gazes steadily in her eyes as he presses one hand against the small of her back, gently pulling her towards him, "I was hungry for food, yet I now have a hunger for something completely different. I've been distracted by your beauty," states Jonathan, with a smile she hasn't seen in quite some time.

His compliments trail into a possible sign of guilt. She smiles at him as she pulls his tie gently from his collar. Jonathan gently lifts her chin up to have her look in his eyes, Jonathan professes, "You know I mean this, don't you? I love you more than anything else in the world. I would be nothing without you, a complete shell of a man. At times, I don't think clearly and I admit I lose focus of what is truly important. I want to make you happy, that is my main purpose in life. You've sacrificed a lot for me and I too intend to do the same for you. That's a promise I won't turn back on."

She smiles and in the moment with all her heart she wants nothing more than to believe him, to have no doubts of his sincerity yet so many years have passed with him making only empty promises. More than anything else, she wants to have faith in him again.

During the course of dinner, Jonathan informs Taylor of some upcoming changes to his normally hectic work schedule, "I have great news. Things are going to slow down for me for awhile beginning next week. I was thinking this would be a perfect opportunity for us to take a much needed vacation; just you and me, with nothing else to interfere."

Taylor's eyes begin to shine along with signs of joy silently expressed on her face, "Oh, Jonathan this is wonderful! We should take a cruise or go to Paris or Greece."

Before he utters a word, she can tell by his eyes, that he isn't open to her vacation locations. He states, "I was thinking more along the lines of a quiet and remote location. We have the villa in Australia and it has been two years since we were there last. With it being cold and bitter here it would be a welcomed change there."

She attempts a smile to conceal her disappointment, all the while not pleased with his proposed destination. Jonathan continues, "Baby, don't you want to get away from the city? We'll have a wonderful time. No phones ringing, no interruptions, just us. We can spend entire days in bed if you'd like, go see some new things on the island, and I don't know about you but I'm thinking a nice little skinny dip in the sea might be something to try. What do you think?"

He smiles, trying to sell her on the idea. Knowing he already has his heart set on it and if she knows him as well as she is certain she does, he has already made the flight arrangements.

With a hint of disappointment still resting in her eyes, she softly replies, "I'm sure it will be fabulous. When do we leave?"

Jonathan gets up from the table and goes over, hugging and kissing her on the neck, "We'll be able to stay for an entire month. I've cleared my schedule. That will give us enough time to get settled and leave plenty of time to have some fun. I've already booked the flight. By this time next week, we'll be heading to sunny Queensland."

The idea briefly stunned Taylor; it was so uncharacteristic of Jonathan, since he wasn't a spontaneous or impulsive type of individual. Spending time on the island wasn't quite the trip she was hoping for, yet she knew it would be wonderful in many ways.

The property itself is exquisite and utterly breathtaking. Jonathan fell in love with the property the moment his eyes caught a glimpse of it on their first visit to the island and he vowed he had to have it, no matter what.

In his usual manner, he knew it would be a great investment and getaway. His set intentions were once he and Taylor reached their golden years, the two of them would move to the island at retirement age, enjoying picturesque sunsets and evening strolls along the beach.

For the first few years, they vacationed there during the summer months, escaping the sounds of busy streets, endless multitudes of people and the hustle and bustle of city life in exchange for a breathtaking atmosphere, tranquility and no interruptions. At these times, it was then the two would find the time and opportunity to rekindle the romance for each other.

Jonathan fancied the villa's location, perfectly set in a lush and wooded area surrounding the house, with the sand reaching up to the back of the property, only yards from the sea; not far from town, yet the closest neighbors' miles away on both sides.

The house itself, reflective of style and innovation has three spacious bedrooms, a master bedroom with its own bath, which includes an onyx wrapped bathtub with gas fireplace just feet away from the tub. The room is complimented by the color scheme of browns and crèmes, with dark walnut floors, giving it a warm and inviting appeal.

The kitchen is spacious with an island complete with a sink, countertops, and a side-bar. The entire inside of the villa has white walls and curtains to draw in light from the outdoors through the large scale windows, opening the inside up to nature's wonderment outside.

Outdoors there is a beach shower, underneath one of many swaying coconut palms that grace the property. The living room faces the backyard with a brilliant view of the translucent sea. The master bedroom is stunning and unique in its own right, with an attached two level tree house off to the side of the bedroom, with its own king sized bed, dressing room, bathroom, a small bar and kitchen, all within screened in walls to catch warm south easterly sea breezes along with a view of the sunset and moon over the Coral Sea.

Taylor begins to remove the dishes from the table, only to have them removed from her hands and placed back in their original place settings upon the table, as Jonathan takes her hands and gazes lovingly and affectionately into her eyes, he tells her, "The dishes can wait. I want to spend some time with you. I've been working constantly and in the process I've neglected you, which I should never do. You are far too important to me. I could never live without you, for my life would not be worth living."

His strong arms holding firmly around her waist: pulling her ever so closely against him, an embrace long since shared between the two. As he caresses her back and neck, she struggles to concentrate on anything else, even once he begins to speak softly to her, "My darling, you are more beautiful and sexier to me now than the day we first met. You drive me wild. I want to kiss every square inch of your body; making love to you throughout the night."

As Taylor focuses on his eyes, seeing the love and sincerity in his gaze, she feels her heart begin to race erratically, as the excitement triggers a chemical euphoria, with instantaneous arousal. He moves in closer, focusing on her lips steadily moving in for a kiss with unbridled passion and force. As they remain locked at the lips, he picks her up making his way into the living room, placing her on the sofa.

With his body hovering over hers, he brushes her hair from her face, kissing her forehead, smiling at her. The longing and yearning for him becomes too much, she urges him along, reaching for his belt, unfastening it. He stops her, softly saying, "No, not like this. I want to make love to you, like I use to."

On the oversized burgundy sofa, Jonathan takes notice to detail and spends the evening pleasuring his wife time and time again. Their bodies intertwined, heat permeating from each other, sweat dripping from their hair, with labored breaths in a continuous rhythm with their lovemaking.

Several times, the intensity overpowers Taylor, as she digs her manicured nails into Jonathan's back, causing him to continue with even more force and exuberance, leading her to ecstasy as she lets out a loud moan.

As the morning daylight filters in the windows, they collapse in each other's arms falling asleep within moments. Peacefully, they cling together, sleeping contently.

CHAPTER 5

FLYING SOLO

OVER THE course of several days, Jonathan persistently works tirelessly to make sure all loose ends are tied up before leaving for Australia, while Taylor cleans out the fridge to get rid of anything that would spoil and packing all their belongings they'll need during their stay.

As it draws closer to the big day, the more excited Taylor finds herself becoming. A real getaway could do them both a world of good. Getting away from all the negative influences and back to the basics could offer them the opportunity of rediscovering all the things that led them to fall in love in the first place.

The night before the scheduled departure, Taylor frantically goes over her various lists, checking to make certain she didn't forget anything; the apartment in immaculate condition for their return, the bags packed and placed near the door, the call ahead to inform the caretaker to prepare the villa for their arrival, the limousine scheduled to pick them up at the apartment and then at the airport in Australia.

As she is going over her list, Jonathan arrives home. Taking his jacket off, placing it along with his briefcase on the chair in the living room. She notices a changed demeanor, not one of a person about to go on vacation, but more like someone bearing disappointing news.

She watches him as he walks towards her with sadness and disappointment in his eyes; he hesitantly says, "Taylor, we need to talk." Without him saying anything else, she knows their trip isn't going to take place, she is certain of that.

Taking her hands in his, Jonathan continues, "Something has come up and it is unavoidable. I would get out of it if at all possible. My case is going to trial sooner than I had planned. I must be here for it. I'm sorry."

Disappointments and let downs are usual occurrences for Taylor, so the news doesn't surprise her in the least, "Its okay, we'll just postpone the trip until your case is settled," says Taylor.

He smiles at her, touching her right cheek gently with the backside of his fingers, "Yeah, I considered doing that, yet it wouldn't be fair to you. Besides, I figure you can go ahead without me and get things set up. I'll only be held up for a few weeks and then I'll join you there. There isn't much point in you waiting around here for me when you can get things accomplished there."

Initially, the idea of traveling so far away and all alone doesn't set well with her, "Jonathan, I don't mind waiting."

He moves in, kissing her brow, "I know you don't, but I truly don't feel as though you should stay and wait. Go ahead without me. I'll call and keep you updated on how everything is going and to let you know how soon I'll be able to join you. With me knowing you're there, it will encourage me to work even harder to get things taken care of here, so I can be with you," he smiles warmly. With reluctance, she agrees to go ahead on her own.

<hr>

All aspects of the journey to Australia are lonely and depressing for Taylor. In all their years of being together, this was the first time she was left to travel alone and to her surprise it was quite frightening, instead of being liberating, as she had hoped it would.

The long plane ride in first class was daunting and dull. The stewardess had offered her some reading materials to keep her occupied, yet she knew she wouldn't be content until she was back on the ground and in a state of control. Having the house to tend to would undoubtedly offer her a sense of purpose.

<hr>

During the limo ride, she takes in the sights, enjoying the beautiful sun shine, fresh air, and the familiar sights. Upon arriving at the villa, she sees the caretaker, Jack Crawford, an elderly man; a native with charm and a wonderful sense of humor. He and his wife live several miles down the road. Jonathan made acquaintances with them when he purchased the property. They obliged to look after the property while it was unoccupied.

She approaches him with a smile, hugging as she reaches him, "Hi, Jack, how are you?"

He squeezes her tightly, laughing, "Mrs. Reed, it is wonderful to see you. The Mrs. and I were pleased to hear you and Mr. Reed made plans to make a stay here. I hope the two of you will be staying for awhile."

Taylor smiles warmly, "For now it is just me, Jonathan will be here in a few weeks. He's anxious to get here."

Jack looks at Taylor with a worried expression on his face, "I hope all is well."

Taylor assures him, "Oh, don't worry. He is just finishing up a case. It isn't anything serious. How is everything here?"

Jack walks with Taylor towards the villa, as the driver takes in her bags, "I have everything set up just as instructed. Your vehicle is in the garage, it has recently been serviced; so it's running in top shape. I have driven it periodically, as Mr. Reed requested. I've been coming up during the day, opening the windows to give it a good airing out. It was quite stuffy, but I think it's quite homey now. You let me or the Mrs. know if there's anything you need," says Jack.

Inside, she looks around taking in her surroundings as if for the first time, since it has been a long time since she last visited the home. Standing a few feet behind, Jack asks, "Mrs. Reed, with your husband back in the States, I can alert the sheriff and have him make rounds in the evenings to make you feel safer. Would you like for me to give him a call?"

Glancing over at him, she says, "Jack, there isn't a reason to do that. No need in troubling the sheriff, he has enough to keep up with without keeping watch on me. I appreciate your concern and all that you've done. The house looks wonderful."

The praise makes the old man smile and blush, knowing how much pride he takes in keeping to detail, keeping to perfection. "If you'd like, I could run into town and do some shopping for you. My Mrs. has me heading that way before returning home and I know your kitchen is bare. It'll save you from having to go out until you've rested."

She contemplates the gesture briefly, "Actually, I think that will be something I'll enjoy doing. I've been cooped up on the airplane for hours. A nice drive to the market will do me good. I do appreciate the offer."

Jack, sensing his requirements are done prepares to leave, "Well, if there's anything I can do, please let me know. My Mrs. will want to have you over for dinner soon, I'm certain of that."

Taylor hugs the little old man, saying, "That sounds lovely. Tell her I'll call her in a day or two once I've gotten settled in. Here's something for giving you such short notice."

She hands him a $100 tip, which he immediately attempts to refuse, "Please take it, I insist. Jonathan and I both know how hard you work keeping this place up and in top shape while we're away, even with what he pays monthly, to me it isn't enough."

The caretaker smiles as he listens to Taylor's nice sentiments, "Mrs. Reed, you and your husband have been most gracious and generous to my wife and me, for the past years we've been fortunate in knowing you both. It is a pleasure to be of service. I'll leave you now so you can get settled in."

Once she is in the house, alone, she begins to contemplate what needs to be done and in what order. The dust covers have already been removed from the furniture. She opens the windows, allowing the gentle breezes to come inside.

The first order of business is toting the bags upstairs to one of the spare bedrooms to store the clothes in one of the spare closets. In a short time, she has everything in place. Quickly, she realizes she is already at a loss in knowing what to do with herself.

Picking up the phone receiver, she calls Jonathan's cell phone and patiently waits as it rings. He answers with no open greeting, "Hi, baby. How was your trip?"

Her soft voice quivers as she replies, "Long and lonely without you; I really wished I had stayed and waited for us to travel together."

Jonathan laughs lightly, "It can't be that bad, besides I'd think you'd enjoy getting away from me for a bit. I know I can drive you crazy at times. Now you have a brief vacation of your own."

Taylor quickly responds, weakness sounding in her voice, "Jonathan, I love you and I assure you I'd much rather be with you. There isn't a great deal for me to do. Jack has taken care of just about everything."

Jonathan's voice rings with warmth, "Darling, it won't be long, I promise and I'll be right there with you. Have some fun, get a little sun and before you know it, we'll be having a fantastic vacation."

Taylor's heart sinks, she begins to feel as if she just might begin to cry, she states, "I miss you."

He can sense the sadness in her tone, "Cheer up, you're beginning to make me feel badly for sending you on ahead of me. I won't be able to rest if I think you're miserable, you know that?"

She makes her best attempt to sound upbeat and cheery, "I'm fine. I have some shopping to do and investigating possible things for us to do once you're here. I'll let you go. I love you."

Jonathan responds with a warm tone, "I love you too. I'll talk to you soon."

⋯⋯

Taylor takes a quick shower, freshening up before heading out to the market. Feeling renewed, she steps out in a close fitted white skirt and buttoned up white long sleeved shirt, with the sleeves rolled half way up and her hair pinned back. Climbing up in the driver's seat of her Lincoln Aviator, she begins to feel a sense of empowerment, losing some of the negativity of being on the island on her own.

As she walks down the market streets, window shopping and smiling at the sight of happy couples and families who are vacationing; briskly, children run playfully down the sidewalks, unaffected by time or responsibility, enjoying their youth. She smiles as they pass her by.

The afternoon sun is bright and warm with the air fresh and clean; unlike back in the city. She could easily become accustomed to living here full time. This would be an ideal place to have a family setting, and a better locality for her to teach: as she still longed to do.

Years ago she had suggested the idea to Jonathan, but was told it would be impossible. The law firms in New York were prestigious and unlike any elsewhere. That was the end of that conversation.

Inside Charlie's Market, Taylor shops for some vegetables and meats for dinner. Pushing her cart along, she pays little attention to those around her and focuses more on the foods in front of her. Polite has always been her manner and speak if spoken to, as with in the city here too she has no friends. She has made Jonathan her primary focus and never questioned that decision.

The truth of the matter is complete isolation doesn't make for a great vacation in such a beautiful part of the world, as Australia. For all intended purposes, she always left the social engagements and business functions up to Jonathan. His jealous streak and demeanor with her conversing with anyone outside of his direction only caused him to become resentful and at times even hostile.

Luckily, at this time of day, the market isn't crowded. Making her way over towards the vegetables, she picks up several tomatoes in search of a few ripe ones, for a nice dinner salad. Unbeknownst to her, a stranger makes his way closer to her, as he too looks at the tomatoes.

He speaks with a mild yet charming British accent, "No matter how often I do my own shopping, I always end up making a disaster of it. I don't suppose I'll ever get the hang of it," says the attractive stranger to Taylor.

Taylor glances at him as he is speaking, thinking he looks like a charming young man. At first glance and observation, she assumes he is in his mid to late twenties, from somewhere in Britain; the accent of course being a distinct giveaway, yet it sounds as if it has its own distinction, maybe from living in another part for awhile.

She takes notice of his brown eyes, how warm and sensual they appear and the moment he smiled she thought immediately how great he looked. Easily he could be one of those catalog models showing off top of the line clothing.

His hair, full with loose curls, mostly at the back running down his neck; it wasn't too long, but enough to have a wildness to it. The thin facial hair, apparently in the early stages, offered a laid back appeal.

From his apparel of tan khaki shorts, black silk dress shirt, brown loafers, and the expensive designer watch suggests he has a well to do job or possibly born into wealth. He smiles at her and she unknowingly begins to smile back.

"It isn't real complicated. I would imagine your profession, what ever it might be, would by far be more complicated to me than the task of shopping," remarks Taylor.

He looks away, grinning, "Yes, you may in fact have a point. Business comes easily to me where smaller and inconsequential things become complex and difficult for me," states the young man.

The stranger smiles again at her, a pleasant smile; his brown eyes seem to come alive with his smile, he continues, "When I'm here, I unfortunately have to attend to my own shopping, or consistently go in search of food, which becomes a bit of a hassle."

Shockingly, Taylor blurts out before thinking it over, "Does your wife or girlfriend not enjoy doing the shopping?" As soon as the words escape her mouth, she drastically wishes she could take them back.

He replies, "I don't have either. I have a few homes, one in London, which is where I mainly hang my hat, which I have the greatest housekeeper who looks after me quite well. She spoils me I must confess, keeping my messes up and making sure I eat well. When I'm here, I vacation alone, so it causes me to be responsible for myself for a change, which is good. I'm sorry, you asked one question and here I am giving you my life's story."

She smiles at the stranger, "Oh, no, please don't apologize. I can understand your plight. Some things are just not easily done alone, and shopping is often one of them," says Taylor. Her eyes mesmerize him, causing him to lose his train of thought.

He smiles, realizing how she has in a split second thrown his concentration just in the gaze of her stunning green eyes, "My name is Alexander Parker III, just about everyone calls me Alex, a bit less formal."

As he holds out his right hand in gesture of a hand shake, Taylor slides her hand gently into his, observing his gentle grasp, "It's nice to meet you, Alex. I'm Taylor Reed."

Alex hesitates for a moment appearing to be considering his next action, he says, "This may sound a bit cliché and forgive me if it comes across in a brash manner, but, would you like to have dinner? There's a great place not far from here, The Desert Moon, do you know it? I, myself, get tired of dining alone. I would enjoy having the company and conversation."

Uneasiness settles in over Taylor abruptly, fearing she has given Alex a misleading impression. Quickly, she heads off any further attempts, haltering any further advances, "Thank you, but I'm sorry I must decline. I'm waiting the arrival of my husband. I do apologize."

Unsuccessfully, Alex conceals his disappointment, as he suddenly discovers her wedding band, feeling a bit foolish he says, "I apologize, I should have noticed your other hand, and I would have had I not been so taken by your eyes."

In that moment her heart begins to speak a language her mind is unable to translate. "It was a pleasure to meet you, Taylor. I do hope you enjoy your stay," says Alex.

She watches as he turns with his basket and walks away, disappearing among other shoppers. With an odd sense of urgency, sensing immediately that she has made a grave mistake in dismissing him and his invitation so hastily. A rapid debate goes on inside her mind wondering if the invitation could have been offered in hopes of establishing a romantic encounter or could it have simply been a friendly gesture? Now, there was no way of being certain.

Before having an opportunity to rationalize what she was about to do, she races through the market with the difficult cart, which appears to be working against her in an attempt to halt her pursuit of the handsome stranger. Just as she is giving up hope of finding him again, she notices him in the dairy section. Her heart beats frantically with each closing step. Never before has such an impulsive motivation taken hold over her, causing her to act with such irrationality.

Standing just inches behind him, she begins to have second thoughts, fearing she is about to make a horrific mistake in judgment. She turns to walk away and in a quick change of heart, turns back towards him just in time to run directly into him. Stumblingly backwards, she looses her balance.

Alex reacts quickly, extending his free arm around her waist, pulling her towards him. His weight firmly planted in place. In that moment, as they stand pressed against each other, only a breath apart, gazing into each other's eyes; Taylor realizes she has forgotten the reason she came in search of him in the first place.

Lost within his captivating brown eyes she feels as though she has been hypnotized and cast under a deep spell, curious as to what lies beneath the sensitive and adorning eyes that are focused upon her so softly.

He asks, "Are you alright? I'm afraid I wasn't looking where I was going."

She regains her balance and composure, feeling a bit awkward and clumsy in her approach, replying; "Yes, I'm fine. I was actually hoping to run into you, at least not literally."

He releases his hand from her waist, she continues, "I was taken back when you invited me to dinner. I admit I was too hasty in my reply and if the offer still exists, I would love to join you."

A smile lights up on Alex's face, "Yes, by all means. That would be wonderful. If you'd like I can pick you up or if you'd prefer, we can meet," says Alex.

Attempting to take it all in as quickly as possible, Taylor contemplates the details, she remarks, "I have been to The Desert Moon once before. I'll meet you there. How is 7:00?"

He shakes his head yes as he agrees, "I'll give you my phone numbers and if something comes up or you change your mind, just give me a ring," states Alex. He pulls out one of his business cards, writing his home and cell number on the back, handing it to her.

They part company again, heading off in opposite directions. As she walks through the market, picking up a few items without paying much regard to what she is picking up, she is overcome by the turn of events, smiling ridiculously. Her behavior was completely so unlike her, acting on impulse had never been a characteristic trait that she possessed; however, she found it to be quite liberating.

For so long, she left decision making up to Jonathan's discretion and in this case, she felt empowered, even if it was just a simple dinner with a polite gentleman. After all, it would be pleasant to have someone to carry on a conversation with for a change. Dining alone had become just a routine as with any other everyday task.

Standing in line at the checkout, waiting her turn to pay for the few items in her cart; she suddenly hears the voice of her distinctive new friend, "I don't know any of these celebrities, do you?" asks Alex.

She smiles as she removes her gaze from the tabloids lined up near the register, to look at Alex, "A few. I don't read these, just glance at the covers. I can think of far better reading material."

Alex gives a short, coy wink, "Let me guess, you like the ever so popular romance novels." She smiles at his quick presumption of her, "Some of them, but mostly I enjoy reading Shakespeare, Plato, Aristotle, Jane Austen and other great works from history's finest."

He appears to be impressed by her interest in classics, "That is quite a reading list. I must admit it is rare to meet one who enjoys reading material often considered to be required material," remarks Alex.

She chuckles, "Oh, a few of them were when I was in college, yet I enjoy them as much now as I did then."

Fascinated by her, he appears eager to find out more about her, he asks, "What was you major in college?"

Placing her items on the conveyer belt, she replies, "It was teaching. I had wanted to become a teacher."

A look of confusion appears on Alex's face, "Wanted to? Did you find it to be more of a challenge than anticipated?"

She replies with a look of sadness in her eyes, "No, due to my husband's career choice, my career has been placed on hold." Halting the conversation she pays for her items.

Alex walks Taylor to her car with both bags in tow, addressing her once they've reached the car, he says, "I don't usually enjoy shopping, but frankly I've thoroughly enjoyed it this afternoon. I do look forward to our dinner engagement this evening. I've greatly enjoyed our market chat, so I have no doubt that our dinner conversation will be just as enjoyable."

Finding herself captivated by his grace and charm, speaking with such elegance and allure; she remarks him to be a true gentleman. As she takes the bag from his arm, their hands briefly touch, offering a slight sense of danger and subtle intrigue. Once in her car, she pulls away slowly, attempting to capture Alex's image one last time before he is completely out of her view. He waves as she pulls away.

At the villa, she puts the market items away, smiling all the while. Suddenly, the phone rings. She answers it briskly, "Hello."

Jonathan's voice sounds from the other end, "Hi, baby, where have you been? I tried calling awhile ago and got no answer. Where were you?"

Calmly she replies, "I made a trip to the market."

He asks, "Who did you go with?"

Taylor replies, "I went alone. Jonathan, what's the matter?"

A moment of hesitation before he responds, "I guess I'm just now realizing I don't like the idea of you being there alone. I should have evaluated the concept a bit more before insisting you go ahead without me. I'm regretting the idea now and think you should have stayed here. You may think I'm being ridiculous."

With a warm, affectionate sounding voice she says to her husband, "Jonathan, you're not being ridiculous. I love that you're concerned and thinking of my welfare. Yes, I would much rather you be here with me, but since you're not, I'm making the best of the situation and I promise you I will not place myself in any danger."

"I have a hectic schedule for the next few days; I won't be able to call you until tomorrow evening. If you need me for anything, call the office and have Jill make certain I get your call. I've already instructed her that it is imperative I get all of your calls," states Jonathan.

She smiles at his simplistic, protective manner, as he says, "I love you. I miss you terribly."

Replying lovingly, she says, "I love you too and miss you more. Win your case so you can get here."

He laughs, "Consider it done, my dear. I have some big plans for us. I won't be able to leave your side for days, I promise you that. I have to go, have sweet dreams. Bye."

CHAPTER 6

DINNER FOR TWO

C ANDLES LIT in the bathroom along with music playing; one of her favorite artists, Brian McKnight, setting the mood while she slips into the shower to get ready for dinner. Taylor begins to feel uplifted and transcended back to a place long forgotten: a time when she felt confident and self assured. The music floats through the house, calming her as she closes her eyes and listens intently:

Love wandered inside
Stronger than you
Stronger than I
And now that it has begun
We cannot turn back
We can only turn into one
I won't ever be too far away to feel you
And I won't hesitate at all
Whenever you call
And I'll always remember
The part of you so tender
I'll be the one to catch your fall
Whenever you call
And I'm truly inspired
Finding my soul
There in your eyes
And you
Have opened my heart
And lifted me inside
By showing me yourself
Undisguised
I won't ever be too far away to feel you
And I won't hesitate at all

Whenever you call
And I'll always remember
The part of you so tender
I'll be the one to catch your fall
Whenever you call
And I will breathe for you each day
Comfort you through all the pain
Gently kiss your fears away
You can turn to me and cry
Always understand that I
Give you all I am inside
I won't ever be too far away to feel you
And I won't hesitate at all
*Whenever you call**

With just an hour to finish getting ready, she looks through her closet for a dress to wear, nothing flashy or provocative. A red crimson dress speaks to her, standing out from the rest. Once on, she looks in the mirror to see it flatter her form and figure perfectly. With the straps fastening together behind her neck, the mid-section holding snug to her breasts and against her waist while the skirt flows to about three inches above her ankles.

After matching the dress with a pair of heels, she looks back in the mirror, focusing intently for any flaws. Her hair, which she curled into wavy ringlets and her makeup soft and subtle, she has the look of a runway model; however, she isn't pleased with her fair complexion.

Spending all her time indoors, she has no color. Wishing she had a few days to gain enough color to look more like a native instead of a tourist, reluctantly she comes to terms there isn't anything that can be done about it now.

Two miles away, down the beach, Alex races from the bathroom to the bedroom, wearing only a bath towel around his waist. His hair dripping wet from the curled ringlets at the base of his neck: streaming down his slender, yet sturdy frame; appearing like rain droplets during a gentle storm.

---

*   Music Lyrics by Brian McKnight

He carefully studies the array of outfits placed across his bed, debating on which to wear. Knowing he doesn't have time to evaluate each one at length, he decides to go with the black dress pants and a black silk shirt.

As he glances at his reflection in the bathroom mirror, he stops to study his appearance. Often he had considered shaving his mustache and goatee, yet it gave him a mature sophistication, which he seemed to lack without it.

In business, having a look of a young kid didn't do much for him in the business sense, due to nobody wanted to take him seriously looking like a inexperienced entrepreneur. Since, after all, this is in fact his vacation; he made the quick decision to shave before meeting Taylor.

Later in the parking lot of the restaurant, Taylor parks her car, glances at herself in the rearview mirror and begins to have second thoughts about the entire thing. She began to wonder if this could be a bad idea. Before now, she hadn't taken the time to reflect on her decision.

The fact being she was already at the restaurant and didn't call to cancel, she felt she had to at least follow through with dinner. Forcing herself from the car, she walks inside the upscale restaurant.

Taking notice of the amazing structural design and the décor, she immediately spots Alex sitting near by in the lobby waiting for her.

He smiles as she approaches, he says, "Hello, you look beautiful this evening."

She smiles briefly, "You look handsome yourself. I'm sorry I'm late."

He brushes off her omission, by informing her, "I just arrived a few minutes ago myself."

As the hostess seats them in a quiet and private spot in a corner, Alex discovers he is beginning to envy a man he doesn't even know. Although he knows little about her, he has instantly become dazzled and captivated by every little detail of Taylor; from her beauty, sophistication, intellect, right down to the lovely fragrance of her perfume.

Taylor gives Alex a quick glance over, finding him striking in all black and admiring his taste and style in fashion. It is apparent he takes interest in the clothing he wears.

Suddenly, she notices something different in his appearance, Taylor remarks, "You look...you shaved! Oh, I so hope you didn't do that on my account."

Fearful that his choice may have in fact been a wrong move, he now wonders if he shouldn't have, he asks; "Did you think I looked better with it?"

Carefully choosing her reply, "It looked quite nice on you; however, I must admit this look has a nice appeal. Of course that is just my opinion and you shouldn't take much from it."

He props his left arm up and without instruction the waiter greets them to take their order. After ordering, Taylor watches Alex as he orders, trying her best not to make her gaze noticeable. She takes in how refined and cultured the young man is, along with his self assurance. He has an air about him, yet it doesn't come across as snobbish or arrogant.

Over the course of dinner, the two hit it off immediately, as if they had known each other for years in place of a few hours. Their discussions stemmed from art, films, cultures, food, childhood aspirations, and even comparing their likes and dislikes. Taylor found herself laughing and smiling more than she has in years. It had been so long since anyone listened to what she had to say as intently as Alex, or even care enough to take an interest.

He studies her intently, watching her body language; in rapture over how lovely every move and mannerism captured her charismatic charm. No matter what the topic, she conveyed herself with such enthusiasm and radiance. While Alex speaks, Taylor listens, fixated on his accent and descriptive account of the most trivial and intriguing revelations.

Alex asks, "Tell me, what you enjoy most about the island that you don't have in New York?"

She hesitates briefly on her reply, "The scenery, I suppose. Traffic, pollution, tall buildings and non-stop noise and commotion surrounding the city, as compared to here; there are busy city areas and not far from that you can find lush nature and unspoiled areas, in its purest element here."

Alex begins, "I agree. When I'm in London, I don't visit the countryside much and after awhile you begin to miss the large green valleys, wide open spaces, and other variables of nature. I've just recently acquired a new estate, which I believe will in time make an excellent getaway retreat."

Curious as to the whereabouts, she inquires, "Where is the estate?"

Lowering his scotch glass back down on the table, "It is an old plantation estate in South Carolina. I'm having it renovated to update sections for current adaptations and having full restorations done to it as well. It is just about complete. I'm quite anxious to see the finished results."

Intrigued she asks, "So what exactly is it you do in acquiring properties? Are these properties you occupy or resale?"

He responds with a smile, "I don't suppose it makes a great deal of sense, yet I buy the properties and for now I occupy them myself. Honestly I don't spend much time at the few I own. I'm rarely here and I'm sure the new property will be just the same. I mainly live at my estate in London, which is where my business is located. I hope to one day have a family and at that time I'll do better at planting roots. Being a bachelor, I can easily live out of a suitcase if needed."

Looking at him warmly, she says; "I think it is wonderful that you have several places to hang your hat. I'm sure the family part will happen in time. Everything has a way of making its own course just as it should."

For Alex, having been around various types of women, he knew how rare and precious it was to come across someone with attributes of beauty and intelligence, with a powerful sense of ones self. In his search for a companion, he searched for those qualities and here before him, Taylor embodied all of those and more. Yet most disappointing she is already spoken for and his search would be forced to continue.

Unaware that time has flown by, making them the last couple within the restaurant, except for a few lingering customers at the bar; Alex takes notice, he remarks; "I believe we are the last ones here and I'm guessing they're hoping we leave soon. I guess we should go." A calm sense overtakes them both as they reluctantly accept the evening is nearing an end.

Walking Taylor to her car, Alex professes to Taylor, "I had a wonderful evening. I must admit I hate to see it come to an end. I'm sure you're exhausted. I've kept you out too late, I do apologize. It has been a long time since I've had someone to carry on a worthy conversation with, one I've enjoyed so much."

Taylor, having enjoyed the evening just as much, if not more briefly ponders the idea before asking, "This is just an idea and feel free to decline, I'd love to take a walk along the beach. It is a beautiful night and while I intended to go for a walk alone, I'd enjoy your company that is if you'd like to join me."

Tickled as well as thrilled at the notion, Alex eagerly agrees without saying a word for the unspoken smile instantly places him in agreement, she says; "I can follow you to your house and we can walk from there."

He politely opens her car door and turns walking a few yards to his black Mercedes, waiting for Taylor to pull up close enough to begin to follow him. Watching in his rearview mirror, he smiles, pleased to have more time to spend with her.

Long ago, his mother had described to him a woman who almost perfectly fit the description of Taylor and how one day their paths would cross when the time was right. Instantly, she said he would know she was the one person he'd spend the rest of his life with, finding love and passion beyond any other.

Of course he was young and was certain she knew nothing of the matter. As he got older he came to believe the idea was an impossible ideal to behold; yet now, her words were coming back to him, as he again had to stop himself reiterating the fact she is unattainable.

Cautiously pulling into Alex's driveway of his beachfront home, stepping from the car, looking at the dim lights leading to the house; she immediately falls in love with the house just with the outside view alone. Large windows, a stunning gazebo located to one side of the house with luscious groomed ivy covering the beams and the sweet fragrance of flowers scattered throughout the immaculate yard.

Alex walks over, standing next to her as she studies the house, he says; "This house said a lot to me before I bought it. I almost didn't."

Unable to imagine anyone passing up on such a great place, she asks, "Why?"

Alex continues, "Well, when the realtor showed it to me, she pressed it being a wonderful environment for a family, I guess assuming I already had one of my own. I could see that vision and felt just maybe the house should be a home to a family. I talked myself out of that and went ahead and bought it anyway."

A spark shines in her eyes, she states; "Good for you. Besides, you shouldn't worry about the family aspect. It will happen for you, I'm sure and until then you can make it into what suits you best."

He brushes his hand through his hair, "I just remembered; my house is a complete disaster. I made a horrific mess of my house earlier as I was getting ready for our dinner date. There are clothes scattered everywhere. I truly would be embarrassed for you to see it. I'd prefer you keep your newly found impression of me a positive one," states Alex.

Taylor giggles, "That's okay. You have not a thing to worry about, especially since I did the very exact thing myself. Who would have guessed the two of us struggled with our wardrobes?"

Alex smiles, feeling a bit more at ease to open his home up, "I suppose there's no harm in going inside." He escorts Taylor inside.

Amazed even more by the inside, she marvels over the spacious and splendid décor of the home, from the black marble floors, rounded archways, white walls offset by the dark colors of black leather furniture in the vast and open living room with a spectacular cathedral ceiling and large scale fireplace. The antique pictures and other pieces give the room an idiosyncratic look and distinct personality. Not the interior she had imagined of a young, single man.

At the far end of the living room; facing the back of the house, beautiful French style doors lead out to a large wooden deck with a perfect view of the Coral Sea: as the moonlight in a cloudless sky dances across the rippling water.

Gazing out at the water, Alex stands behind unable to notice the beauty of the evenings natural wonder, for the beauty before him he is unable to draw his eyes away from. "Alex, you have a lovely home. I absolutely adore everything about it."

Alex replies, "Thank you."

She turns to him, "I'm far more impressed with your home than my own. The villa is nice but it is far too large. It is a mere waste. I love what you've done with the interior; I think ones décor reflects the personality of its owner, expressing individuality and uniqueness. It has such a warm and inviting feeling."

As Taylor walks over to the large windows near a sitting room, looking out at the night's sky, Alex follows, he says; "You sound as if you're experienced in decorating."

She tilts her head, remarking; "I don't really. My friend, Shannon, took interior design in college. She is a clothing designer now. I managed to pick up a few things during her studies. It is such a beautiful evening. Not a cloud in the sky."

Alex motions towards the kitchen, "Could I interest you in a glass of wine? I have a few bottles that I brought back from Italy a few years ago."

Gazing at him with a spark of interest, she responds; "Yes, I'd like that." He looks at her intently, "I'll get the wine and glasses. You can head out to the back deck if you'd like."

As Alex is in the kitchen, Taylor further studies the room, glancing at an array of photographs in frames along the end tables and mantle piece. A few of the pictures are baby portraits, which she assumes are family members.

Handing her a glass of wine, "That one you're looking at is yours truly. I was a plump baby. Thankfully, as I got older and became more active, I lost the baby fat. This one here is of my mum and me when I graduated from college. She was so proud of me on that day. These here, are my cousins, Jeffrey, Sabrina, and Matthew."

She marvels at the picturesque family photos, "You come from such happy roots. That's a wonderful thing," says Taylor.

He senses a somber mood in her tone, as he asks, "Were your roots not happy ones?"

An unhappy expression comes across her face, which she changes up immediately, as she continues; "A long time ago. My father died seven years ago and I don't see my family much any more. My mother moved to Florida, remarried, and she utterly despises my husband. I'm an only child, so I don't have any siblings. I don't want to depress you with my gloomy family stories. May I have a tour of your lovely home?"

Alex hesitates momentarily, feeling compassionate for Taylor wondering how an individual could do nothing else but deliver all that is glorious and magical to such a pure and divine individual, like herself.

"Yes, I'd be happy to show you around. You'll have the grand tour. I just hope I haven't left too much mess lying around. I'm not the world's greatest housekeeper, especially when I'm left to fend for myself," states Alex.

He smiles and begins to lead the way to show her around the house. Looking around, she finds each and every room unique and mesmerizing with its own unique style and flare. The detail implies he took a great deal of effort in decorating each room, creating his own vision into a reality.

In the master bedroom, they venture inside standing a few feet from each other. As Taylor admires the brilliant splendor of the room, from the large-scale full length wall windows, opening one entire side up to a picturesque view of the sea to the massive cherry poster bed resting on a raised stair leveled floor; Alex becomes transported to a vision, pulling Taylor close, holding her tightly all the while kissing her ever so passionately.

The urge takes over to whisk her up, place her on the bed, make passionate love to her and spend the rest of the night holding her in his arms in a loving embrace; then in the morning, waking to the reality of her presence still with him.

Lost in his vision, Taylor attempts to ask a question, "Don't you absolutely love the view?"

Realizing he has missed what she said he asks reluctantly, "I'm sorry."

She looks at him, "The view, it is breathtaking."

He replies; "Oh, yes it is, especially this evening. We'll sit on the deck for a bit, if you'd like."

Sitting outside on the outdoor loveseat, feeling the warm, gentle breeze flowing across the moonlit sky, the two enjoy their wine and talk like old friends catching up on lost times would.

"This wine is extraordinary. I've never had anything quite like this. Would you mind telling me of the time you spent in Italy? I've always wanted to travel there," says Taylor.

Placing his wine glass down, turning to face her, he begins "I'm certain you would love it. It is quite a moving experience, one you'll never forget. You get a sense of being transcended to another time, a place so full of history and a timelessness that can't be found anywhere else. I can do my best to describe it to you, yet I know I won't do it justice. There, you find yourself lost from everything else you know; it has such evanesce. The history and landscape are so surreal."

She hangs on every word he utters, attempting to envision herself in such a majestic place. She ponders over the idea how magical it would be to travel to foreign lands, evoking romance and passion from within a special relationship.

With no hesitation she asks, "Did you fall in love while you were in Italy?"

Her question causes him to laugh before quickly offering a smile, "No, I didn't. It would have been an absolutely perfect place to be in love. I'm certain when the time is right, love will finally find me, besides I believe it would be far greater to take love to Italy; than to be there attempting to seek it out."

His openness and admissions interests her, eagerly causing her to want to learn as much as she can about him as much as the remaining evening will allow. She proceeds to inquire further, asking; "Have you ever been married?"

Alex begins to wonder what motivation lies behind her line of questioning, he answers; "No, not ever close. I've made a point of focusing solely on my career and in all honesty, behaving as young bachelors often do. For me, I have to know my head is in the right place and I know once I begin my search for my soul mate it will be a top priority."

His ideas in finding his soul mate seem calculated and detailed, which confuses her, she asks quizzically "What if you wait for a soul mate that doesn't exist or she passes you by? You could miss out on finding her. I don't think it can be entirely left to chance; you have to be willing to put the time in to find who's right and who's wrong. You can enter a relationship, which appears to be heaven sent and after time passes, you may be surprised to discover it wasn't destiny or a fairytale, but a union that wasn't meant to be after all."

Her pessimistic view, along with the sense of speaking from first hand experience, doesn't go overlooked as Alex smiles sympathetically; "I have faith and hopes that when the time is right for me, I'll know it without question. Destiny will steer us in the same direction. I'm strongly relying upon my heart to tell me. Once I embark on finding my other half, I'll turn my life upside down to do all in my power to make her happy for the rest of my life."

Unbeknownst to her, Taylor loses herself in her thoughts at the end of Alex's statement. The gaze of her eyes appears stunned or dazed, staring off as though frozen in time. Alex, uncertain of what to do or say, waits momentarily in hopes that she'll speak or blink.

As if woken from a spell, she returns to her normal demeanor and smiles at him, "Alex, you're remarkable. I've never met anyone quite like you with such admirable insights and standards. Whomever this person turns out to be, I assure you she will be very lucky and I just hope she'll see that for herself."

Flattered by her compliment, his eyes look upon her gently, he says; "I must confess, you're the first person I've met in a long time, so finding Mrs. Right might be awhile yet. For the most part, I stay absorbed in my work and I do a great deal of traveling. I don't make romance an easy aspect and on the rare occasions I meet someone to take to dinner, it doesn't develop into anything further due to not having the time to invest in giving it room to grow. I notice I get more depressed about it at certain times and that's when I begin to wonder if I'm destined to spend my life alone."

She rests her right hand gently just above his left kneecap, with a soft expression she offers him encouragement, "Don't think that way. It will happen for you. If you give up hope and on finding love in general, you won't see it even if it's standing right in front of you," says Taylor.

As he looks deep into her eyes, he thinks to himself of the sensation he has already felt from the moment he saw her in the market. His intuition told him this lovely lady is special in many aspects. He knew he needed no proof of this.

Without a doubt and all certainty, he would cross the line if he were only able; for his longing and driving desire to sweep her up in his arms and carry her off into a life of forever. Yet he knew his impulses had to be denied and overcome.

Caught up in the moment, as she gazes out to the sea watching the moonlight dance across the rippling water, Alex is lost in the touch of her hand on his leg. Her beautiful, jeweled emerald green eyes mesmerize him with each glance.

Everything about her exemplifies perfection, from her wavy brown hair, slender form, soft, white skin. Her smile is most notable for it causes the warmest sensation when seen. If only he could be the one to keep her smiling all the time.

He wouldn't have her do anything else, never do anything to see sadness in her eyes or smile. The endless tug of war battle goes on within between his mind and heart. With every fiber of his being, he knows she is the one he has searched for and the one he'd love nothing more than to make a future together.

As Alex looks out at the night's sky, Taylor cautiously moves her hand, noticing for the first time where she unknowingly placed it. She says, "Alex, tell me about your family."

He looks back at her, smiling favorably, "My father was a prominent figure in Britain. Both he and my mum came from wealthy heritages. I went to boarding school and attended Princeton. Business is what I was surrounded by growing up, so needless to say, I know little else."

Giggling briefly, she asks; "Are you saying you never got into any kind of mischief?"

He looks at her quizzically, "Who, me?" He laughs, as he continues; "I had my fair share of getting in trouble when I was younger and like most boys, I had a rebellious streak. My father didn't let me get by with much, which I can honestly say now, I'm grateful for because it gave me a bigger sense of purpose."

She interjects, "I'm sure your family is very proud of you and all you've accomplished at such a young age."

Alex refreshes her glass as he continues, "My mum is and I suppose my father was before passing away a few years ago."

Compassion shows in her eyes, "Alex, I'm so sorry."

Alex continues, "I was always struggling to gain my father's approval in every way possible. He wasn't the easiest person to impress. For him, being the man he was, it caused me to strive to do my very best and if he thought I was capable of more, it gave me an opportunity to look closely at myself, to judge on my own if I gave it all I had or not. I truthfully don't think I'd be where I'm at today without that sharp eye for detail or the encouragement to excel."

As the temperature begins to change, becoming cooler, Alex pulls a blanket out from the storage bench near the swing, covering Taylor with it. Immediately, she takes part of it and covers him too.

Huddled up together; Alex places his arm around Taylor, careful not to hold too tightly against her. They watch the night's sky and in a short time of silence, Alex asks, "Is the night air getting too cool for you?" He waits for a reply and doesn't get one.

He peers over to see Taylor has fallen asleep with her head resting inside his shoulder.

He ponders over whether he should wake her and decides for the moment, to indulge his selfish satisfaction of having her nuzzled against him. After some time has passed, Alex carefully picks her up with precision and delicately carries her into the house, placing her on the sofa in front of the fireplace.

She moves a little as he lays her down. Bending down by her side, he gazes at her lovingly, covering her up and gently brushing her hair away from her face. As he watches her sleep, noting her steady and rhythmic breathing, along with her angelic appearance; he smiles at the sight before him. She embodies so much purity and warmth; he is overcome and even quite shaken by it.

Before she entered his life, he felt as though nothing was amiss in his world. His priorities were laid out before him, but now it was all so different and various questions had now begun to confuse him: wondering had he been truly happy or if this is what it feels like to be in love.

He considers waking her, but doesn't want to disrupt her peaceful sleep. With dawn just a few hours away, he is certain she is completely exhausted so he just decides to let her sleep. Not wanting her to wake in a strange place and become alarmed, he curls up on the matching sofa beside her, watching her intently until he too drifts off to sleep.

CHAPTER 7

A NEW LEASE ON LIFE

A s THE early morning sunlight dances across the water its rays of light bounce off the windows illuminating sparkling crystals of light throughout the house. Taylor wakes, struggling to recall where she is and exactly how she got here.

Taking a quick glance about the room, she suddenly comes across a familiarity, Alex lies sleeping on the other sofa. She smiles and begins to wonder how the evening ended. She could recall the two of them talking and the warmth they shared between them under the blanket, causing her to feel completely comfortable. She had no recollection of falling asleep.

Knowing she really must leave, she quietly tiptoes over to where Alex continues to enjoy the realm of sleep, with her voice ever so gently calling out to him, "Alex". He stirs briefly, still deep in sleep. Gently she caresses his cheek and whispers, "Alex, wake up. Open your eyes."

Slowly, his eyes open immediately focused on her. He feels Taylor's warm breath on his face, with the lingering aroma of the wine still resting on her breath. She looks troubled or worried, he asks, "Is everything okay? What's wrong?"

She begins, "I'm sorry, Alex, about falling asleep. Please forgive me; I had no intentions of being such a rude guest. I'm truly sorry."

A sense of relief causes him to laugh abruptly, "Please, don't apologize. I had the greatest time. I'll admit at first I considered that I possibly put you to sleep with my boring conversation, but the reality of us staying up until the wee hours of the morning convinced me that was root of the cause."

Smiling at her in a way, which instantaneously causes her to smile at him in return, he continues, "Besides, it may sound a bit corny or even childish, I enjoyed the simplicity of watching you sleep, I couldn't bring myself to wake you."

Feeling her heart warm inside her chest, thinking just how much she enjoys hearing the boast and brag with admiration, yet it isn't coming from the person it should be, her husband. Alex gets up, "I can prepare breakfast. I'm sorry to say I'm not great at it but I can manage eggs and toast."

As though suddenly realizing she is late for something or Cinderella who has just heard the clock strike midnight, fearing that all that was good will immediately vanish forever, she hesitates, saying "Alex, that sounds lovely, but I'm afraid I must go."

Attempting to appear as though he isn't disappointed, not quite convincing at it either, he replies, "Oh, I understand; I took up far too much of your time--"

She quickly interjects, "No, Alex, not at all. You misunderstand; I do in fact have errands I must take care of. I greatly enjoyed our evening and I too hate to see it come to an end, yet I really must go."

A smile returns to his face, "Do you have plans for lunch?"

She smiles, "With you. I'll give you a call and we'll plan out the details."

Picking up her shoes from the floor, she kisses Alex softly on the cheek before leaving.

Over the course of the morning, Taylor discovers she is unable to stop herself from smiling, fixated on pure joy. A sense of rejuvenation and awakening has occurred, offering a new lease on life.

Impatiently she waits for the afternoon to arrive, anxious to see Alex once again. Soaking in a warm, bubble bath the phone rings startling her from reevaluating thoughts of the night before. Anxiously she steps from the tub, racing to the phone barely having enough time to cover herself with a towel.

Her intuition tells her it's Alex, she grabs for the receiver, clumsily lifting it up, just about dropping it to the floor; nervously and anxiously answering, "Hello."

Jonathan's impatient tone sounds off, "Taylor, what's going on? Why are you out of breath?"

She responds, "Jonathan, I was in the bath when the phone rang. I raced to the phone."

His tone heightens with jealousy, "Were you expecting someone else to call?"

"Of course not, Jonathan, why would you ask such a thing?"

He pauses and the silence sends chills throughout Taylor, "I'm not comfortable with you being there alone. It was a mistake in my sending you ahead without me."

Taylor feels resentment and anger in his implication, "I can't believe you're saying this to me. I was willing to stay and wait while you insisted I go alone. What would you like for me to do, come home?"

He responds with a burden of guilt tone in his voice, "Yes, I know I asked you to go on without me, yet I don't like the idea of you being there alone. It is unfamiliar country and being a female, there alone isn't a good thing. You know how I can get."

The truth was she did in fact know how he could get. Early in their relationship, he had shown no jealous tendencies and then as time passed his jealous streak reared its ugly head far more times than she willingly wanted to admit.

She knew his fears and past relationships fueled his insecurities, yet no matter how she would strive to convince him of her undying love, he always managed to second guess her feelings and emotions for him.

She replies to his remark, "I can take care of myself--"

Quick to interject, he states cautiously, "Taylor, I'm not implying that you can't, I just would feel better knowing that my wife is being looked after and safe. I'm too far away to be able to do anything if it were needed. I couldn't live with myself if anything were to happen to you, can you understand that?"

Displeased with the direction the conversation is going, she desperately tries to change the subject, "How are things there?" "Taylor, I'm thinking of your well-being. I would kill myself if anything happened to you."

Disturbed by his claim of self-inflicting death, she quickly reassures him, "Jonathan, please don't say things like that. I don't like hearing you say those kinds of things. I'm not going anywhere that is unfamiliar to me. Please try not to worry. You'll be here soon."

He begins to sound a bit more uplifted, "I'm sure you're right and I'm likely overreacting as usual. I miss you so very much. I can't recall the last time we were apart like this. I assure you; as soon as I arrive we'll spend an entire 24 hours in bed together. I won't be able to let you out of my sight."

At the end of their call, she begins to contemplate everything from the way she currently feels, to what she is doing, and even the possible outcome. Taking into consideration, she could never be a friend with Alex and they would certainly never be able to speak once Jonathan arrived and heaven forbid if he stumbled across their brief acquaintance, for that would prove to be disastrous.

Jonathan, being the proud, controlling and dominating man he has always been, would never place himself in the position of becoming a victim, oh no; he would reverse the situation entirely. He would make Alex wish he had never set eyes upon his wife, lighting into him like the tooth and nail defense attorney he is known so well for.

As for Taylor, that would be a completely different scenario. She would be the actual victim; she would feel heartbroken over inflicting such devastating effects upon Alex, all the while her husband would make certain she would never forget the tumultuous mistakes she made.

Lashing out and beating her would not be totally out of the question, it would most certainly be expected. Submission would be the intended result; to beat her like an unloved dog, making her crawl back, wearily and cautiously at his heels; willing to do anything and everything to make good for what she did to cross him.

With the thoughts and visions plaguing her mind, making the idea of spending the afternoon with Alex a bad idea, she finds herself struggling to make a solid decision either way. Her heart desperately wants her to go while her better judgment tells her to break it off now while there is time.

The phone rings, she answers without clearing her mind, "Hello."

Alex's voice sounds over the line, "Hi, I thought I'd give you a call. I wanted to ask if you'd like to go for a drive this afternoon. I'm not well equipped on making plans that include more than me." She doesn't respond.

Concern sounds in his voice, "Taylor, is everything all right? Is this a bad time?"

Forcing herself back to the conversation, she responds, "No, I'm sorry; I'm just a bit distracted. Umm, a drive would be lovely. What time should we meet?"

He responds with hesitation, "12:30. I have a few things to do first. I don't want to be presumptuous or out of line, but if this is uncomfortable or places you in a bad position, we can cancel."

Her heart races, "No! Alex, it doesn't. I really want to see you."

Anxiously he replies, "Okay, come by at 12:30 and I promise you a great afternoon. I'll see you in a bit." Hanging up the phone, she bites down on her bottom lip still debating on the decision she has just made.

Back in New York, Jonathan sits quietly at his desk in his large and impressive office, blankly gazing at the photo of his wife on top of his desk. Jill, knowing her boss can be charming and debonair and yet at times harsh and stuffy; she is careful in approaching him. "Mr. Reed." He doesn't take notice of her or respond, "Mr. Reed, I'm sorry to interrupt you but you have a meeting with Mr. Calhoun in ten minutes."

He stares at her with a wild look of negativity, one she can't decide if it's evil or just pure hatred. It immediately causes her to stop dead in her tracks, like a deer struck by blinding headlights. She takes a deep breath, "Mr. Reed, is something wrong?"

His gaze stays on her for a moment longer before he looks away, stating coolly; "I need for you to contact the florist I use in Australia and have a large bouquet of red and black roses sent to my wife. The card should simply read, "Thinking of you. We'll be together real soon. Love, Jonathan."

Fearing her boss's current demeanor, she hesitates briefly before repeating the order back to him, "Okay, that's a bouquet of red and black roses?"

He stands and walks towards her, gazing with the same inexplicable evil as he had before, "Yes, Jill, that's right. After my meeting, I'll be out for lunch. I won't be back in the office until 2:00. Take messages and call me only if it's an emergency. You can go."

Jill quickly returns to the safety of her desk.

Before heading out for his scheduled meeting, he picks the photograph of Taylor up and looks at it, caressing the glass placed over her smiling face, reassuring himself, "Just a reminder that you don't mess with me. No man will ever have you, but me. I'll make certain of that. If anyone ever makes a move on you, I'll find out and I guarantee he'll never be able to do the same ever again. You're my greatest possession and all that I do is simply for you. If you ever betray me, I'll make you sorry. It will cost you dearly, that I promise."

He walks towards Rex Calhoun's secretary, Janet, an old slender woman in her fifties who has worked for the same boss for twenty years.

Jonathan, with his bright smile and cheery demeanor asks, "Janet is he ready?" She smiles back at the handsome attorney standing before her, "He is, go on in he's expecting you."

Inside the large scale office, much larger than Jonathan's, Rex notices him and stands to shake hands to greet the brilliant attorney who has brought further prosperity to the firm; he says, "There's my top attorney. I keep abreast to all the latest news and I have heard of your extraordinary work, which I'm delighted with. Keep up the excellent work my boy and you'll soon find yourself partner here. Your current client is raving about your capabilities. He is pleased with the progress."

Jonathan smiles, "Thank you sir. I've worked very hard to get where I am. Reaching the top has driven me the entire way. Becoming a partner is the greatest accomplishment I could ever have the honor of receiving."

Mr. Calhoun sits back down, signaling Jonathan to do the same, "Let's not forget about that beautiful wife of yours, she is a wonderful gem. How is she?"

Discussing his wife isn't a conversation piece he wishes to pursue, yet he unwillingly replies, "Oh, she's well. She is in Australia at our vacation home. I will be joining her there once the case is settled."

Rex continues, "I'm sure she misses you terribly; just as you miss her. To be young and in love again, it is such a wonderful thing. I can't say I remember the feeling that well. It has been a long time since my wife and I have done anything of a romantic nature. In all sincerity, our marriage is more or less convenience. She does her thing and I do mine. That is something you'll hopefully never have to face. You have a devoted and loving wife who adores you. Tell the little lady I said hello the next time you speak."

Feeling even more insecure and uncomfortable, he forces a smile, "I certainly will. What did you want to discuss?"

Without hesitation Mr. Calhoun begins, "I think you know of Ronald Ewing, the high powered French entrepreneur. He is throwing a party this weekend. He has dropped your name and insists that you attend. It is a black tie event by invitation only. This function is going to have endless top executives and foreign big names. You need to work them up. There is a potential to gain some respective clients. Do this and we'll see about getting Judge Ramey to speed up your case, so you can get to that pretty wife of yours a lot quicker."

Jonathan despises his boss's pawning and deceptive ways of getting things done. Knowing he has no possibility of refusing, he agrees, "You've got yourself a deal."

Back in Australia, Taylor enjoys a scenic ride with Alex as he drives to a beautiful nature trail spot. Turning the ignition off, quietly he gazes off in the direction in front of him beginning to speak before turning his gaze to Taylor, "I know this is not my place, but I do understand you're married and while what we're doing is completely innocent, to others it may not appear that way. I must confess I've instantly become taken with you although we've only just met. I don't want to see you distressed or worried over the consequences of us spending time together. I want you to know that I'll completely understand if you wish to stop spending time together."

She looks at him warmly as a smile lights up her face, "Thank you. I am concerned that I'm doing an injustice to my husband by spending time with you, when the fact is it won't be long and we'll have to part ways. My husband would not be comfortable with us conversing. You are a wonderful person, Alex, and I'm so happy we met, I just don't want to complicate things for you and my life is often complicated," says Taylor.

Alex grins with a slight twinkle in his eyes, "Don't worry about me. I too am grateful for meeting you. My vacation would be less interesting and to be quite honest, a bore without having someone like you to enlighten it. When the time comes, we'll part ways and just enjoy each other's company and the times we were fortunate to have. This here is a wonderful trail. I've walked it once before. It leads out to the water. Have you been here before?"

She looks out at the area, "No, I haven't. Sadly there are a lot of great places I haven't seen here."

Removing the key from the ignition, he asks, "What do you say, want to go on the trail with me?"

Smiling, feeling a rush of adrenaline, she replies, "I'd love to."

Together they walk along the spectacular trail, taking in one of the world's most variable trails enjoying the lush plant life which opens up to a breathtaking view of the sea. As the large forest hovers over them, leading out towards the end of the trail, they separate from two other couples that walk on ahead; Taylor professes, "I don't think I've ever seen anything this beautiful before. It is so stunning."

Alex looks at her, "Yes, indeed, stunning." She notices he is looking at her when he says it, causing her to blush.

With a brief moment of consideration, he inquires, "May I ask about your husband?"

The idea of detailing Jonathan is not a topic she'd care to embark on, yet she feels a sense to oblige, "What about him?" Her voice trails off quietly.

Alex responds, "Well, I guess I'm curious as to what types of qualities such a lucky man, as himself, possesses."

With a deep breath, she describes him the best she can and offering the briefest summary possible, "Jonathan is extremely goal-oriented, a bright and brilliant defense attorney, a wonderful husband."

Alex continues with questions in a subtle tone, asking "How did the two of you meet?"

Rushing into her response, "We met in college, began dating, and moved in together after graduation and soon after married."

He is able to sense awkwardness in her reply, finding that he regrets the inquiry, "I'm sorry, I shouldn't have asked so many questions. It was rude of me and none of my business please forgive me for doing so."

With her eyes expressing a more lightened demeanor, she states, "No, it's alright. I don't usually discuss my husband and to speak of him in depth wouldn't necessarily place him in the most positive of light. He has wonderful qualities and he also has some not so flattering attributes. Our marriage has encountered a good deal of downs lately, but I'm hopeful that things will turn around once again."

Alex smiles, "I'm sure it will."

Both follow the trail out the rest of the way, near the water. The view is glorious, with a bright blue sky, the sun passing mid-day and the sea shifting back and forth. Off in the distance, Alex spots a sailboat.

He leans close behind Taylor, whispering in her left ear as he points over her right shoulder to the sailboat, "There's a boat, somewhat like my own. This is a fabulous day for sailing. I should've thought of it myself."

Turning to look at him; misjudging the closeness of their proximity, closely coming within centimeters of his lips. Quickly, she backs up, forgetting what she was about to say.

He studies her for a moment, "Taylor, were you going to say something?" He begins to look at her with a quizzical brow.

Taylor struggles to recall the thought that was so very present before almost brushing into a kiss with Alex; which instantly had the distracting effect. She continues once able to return from the spell, with unbridled enthusiasm she states, "Oh, I was going to say I'd love to go sailing with you. I've never been on a boat. I imagine it would be a great experience."

Taking her hand in a friendly gesture, he says, "It's a certainty then, I promise."

An older couple, standing a few feet away from them; the old lady says, "It is so nice to see such a loving young couple, like you two, embracing nature together. It reminds me of when my husband and I were much younger. You can easily tell, just by looking at the two of you that you're soul mates and what a terrific connection you share."

Alex and Taylor smile at each other, both sensing they can't mislead the woman's take on the situation, when she is nowhere near the actual truth. Alex remarks to the old lady, "Thank you that means a lot. We can only hope to be as happy as you two when we have been together the same length of time."

As the older couple walks away, Taylor and Alex both can't hold back their laughter at being mistaken for a couple. They walk hand in hand back towards the car, jokingly calling one another hubby and wife.

During the course of the evening, Taylor having invited Alex to join her at the villa for dinner, the two begin talking while she is in the kitchen preparing dinner. The night air is warm with a slight breeze, carrying the sweet fragrance of exotic flowers from outside; filtering through the sheer full length drapes. Soft and dim lighting compliments their faces, illuminating sensual qualities in each other.

He studies her ever so carefully watching each minute thing she does, from washing the vegetables in the sink to the way her hair flows gently over her shoulder, running down her back. The lovely one piece white summer dress she wears flows softly down her shapely form.

Over the course of dinner, the two talk casually. With the desire to learn all he can about this woman he finds completely fascinating, he asks, "Let me see if I can guess what you were like as a child."

He gives deep thought and concentration, pondering it briefly before giving his reply, "I imagine you were a quiet and gentle person, made your observations of others yet not posting your opinions or views as most would. You've encountered a life of sporadic disappointments at the hands of others, causing you to be cautious at trusting others initially. You have a keen sense of character and self, which I imagine has for the most part not led you astray. How am I doing?"

Briefly she appears to be caught in a trance and then coolly comments, "You have a very good insight into who I am, which I must admit I find to be intriguing due to our short acquaintance."

He adds, "I have studied you ever so studiously from the first moment I saw you in the market. You hypnotized me instantly with your beauty, charm, grace and humor."

With a slight giggle and flush in her cheeks, she says, "Alex, you flatter me with your compliments; however, I'm not certain I can claim such amiable qualities. By no means do I behold any ounce of perfection as you so willingly address."

Alex looks at Taylor with a sheer luster of confidence that she does in fact obtain such strong and unpretentious qualities, "Would you care to give me a shot? What is your observation of me?" As he focuses intently on her eyes, she smiles with her eyes expressing warmth and softness, as she begins to detail her insight into the character of Alex Parker.

She looks in his eyes, beginning with her reflection, "I believe you are a warm and charismatic young man with creativity, hard work and lusting after change you have thus far been unable to obtain in your life. You had to grow up too quickly, taking on responsibilities before you wished to, yet you did it with such a zealous and courageous exuberance to impress your family and gain the respect from those who didn't believe you had it in you. You're at a point where you wish to find love and have someone to share your life's experiences with, to build a future instead of a path of loneliness and solitude."

In that moment, surprisingly Taylor hits closer to home than Alex was prepared to hear. The smile fades from his face as the realism of her words has planted a blow to his self-esteem that he can't immediately bounce back from. It had always been a difficult subject but to hear it from Taylor made it seem all the more horrible, shedding a spotlight on his flaws and unattainable dreams.

Taking one of her hands in his, he bends over slightly to kiss it, speaking quietly, "I've had a wonderful time with you today and I thank you for dinner. I must be going, it's getting late."

Afraid she has insulted him, trampling on his ego, she pleads, "Oh, Alex, I apologize. I didn't have any intentions of saying anything that offense would be taken to. Please, I'm certain I was anything but right. You don't have to go."

He smiles, still appearing wounded, "You didn't offend me. What you said was the complete truth and is something I think about on a daily basis, for it is something I greatly long to change and I have hope that one day I will. I'm not leaving over anything you said, please believe me. It is late and I think best to call it a night. We'll get together tomorrow if you'd like. You can give me a call."

He kisses her hands again and leaves. She watches at the window as he walks to his car, sullenly and drives away. Her heart goes out to him as she finds she wants to comfort and reassure him. If it were up to her, she'd make certain he never had to spend another day alone again.

CHAPTER 8

THE FEAR FACTOR

Taylor rises to a beautiful, sunny morning. She eagerly begins making plans for her day, deciding to make amends for the negativity she unleashed during dinner the night before by surprising Alex with a day planned entirely by her.

As she begins to look in her closet for something to wear, the doorbell rings. Immediately, sensing Alex is at the door, she races downstairs in her blue shorts and t-shirt, pulling the door open with a smile on her face; ready to welcome him.

To her surprise, it isn't Alex but a delivery man holding the most heinous and despicable bouquet of flowers she has ever seen. The black roses turn the red ones into pure evil. The delivery man holds the vase of two dozen red and black roses surrounded with baby's breath, "I have a delivery for Mrs. Taylor Reed," says the delivery driver.

Her pulse races and her heart begins to feel as if it has missed several beats, her voice breaks as she answers, "I'm Taylor Reed."

The young man starts laughing, "Wow, I expected you to be like 40, you know, over the hill with the black roses and all. Someone pulled a cruel joke on you, huh?"

Unable to locate the words all she can do is nod.

Unwillingly she takes the flowers inside, placing them on a table, carefully removing the card. Her hands shake with fear as she struggles to open the small envelope, delicately removing it as if it were a bomb ready to detonate upon touch. Chills run down her spine as she opens and reads the card. Although miles and miles away from one another; Jonathan knows exactly how to control and manipulate her with the greatest of ease.

Instantly the tears begin to roll down her cheeks as she reads the contemptible note. She stares at the flowers feeling vulnerable, in an attempt to regain her confidence and control, she whisks the vase up violently from the table and towards the fireplace, where she tosses them into the blazing fire; watching them burn.

Sadly this wasn't Jonathan's first display of evil and hostility. Over the course of their marriage he has carried out various contemptuous attacks towards Taylor, such as taking one of her beloved paintings slashing it beyond recognition. The most vengeful act was when he took the kitten away he gave as a birthday gift, accusing it of tearing up his ties which was completely untrue.

Unbeknownst to her, it was in fact her husband who was the one responsible for each and every rejection letter to all of the teaching jobs she has applied for time and time again. He single handedly intervened before any of them could be offered, of the multitudes of schools that desperately wanted her on their staff.

At this stage, his antics seemed second nature. She is still hurt by his callous ways, yet she shrugs it off and does her best to forget about his immaturity. Determined not to allow Jonathan's actions the capability to dampen the rest of her day, she gets dressed; wearing a pair of jean shorts, a thin-strapped red halter top blouse and white tennis shoes. Her hair still damp, it drips from the tips down her neck. Quickly she grabs her towel to catch the droplets before they drench her clothes.

The doorbell rings and immediately her heart skips a beat as a sudden rush of fear takes hold. Cautiously, she walks towards the door, opening it slowly. At first, all she can see from the small amount she has allowed of the open door, is a large bouquet of beautiful red, pink and white roses; concealing the carrier.

Never before had Jonathan done something so terrible only to quickly make amends. This could in fact be a first; she thought as a voice sounds from behind the flowers, "I hope you'll accept these flowers and my sincerest apology. I feel utterly terrible about how I've behaved." The voice is not that of her husband, but Alex.

Taking the bouquet of flowers from him, revealing his dashing face and his attire of black khaki shorts and a relaxed white button up shirt, partially unbuttoned. For a moment, she forgets what she was about to say as she remains lost in a trance of his masculine appeal; from his toned legs, island tan, and the way his hair curls naturally causing her to want to just run her hands through it.

Smiling at him, she says, "Alex, you don't owe me an apology. The flowers are simply lovely, thank you so much. The fact of the matter is I was just heading out to come over to apologize to you."

He looks at her peculiarly, as if confused, "Whatever for?"

Removing flowers from a vase on the table in the open corridor, placing the roses in place of them, "I behaved so poorly last night. My manners completely left me. I honestly wouldn't blame you if you decided never to see me again."

He lets out a laugh, "I would never be foolish enough to cost myself your company. I'm having a blast with you."

She feels her heart soar, beaming with joy, she states, "Please come inside, and let me find the perfect place for these beautiful flowers."

He steps inside and takes a glance, where he stands, of the inside, "This house is truly magnificent. It has a great deal of character and its own unique attributes."

She enters the entranceway near Alex, "Would you like a tour?"

Struggling to refrain from staring at her, yet unable to lose sight of her beauty, he replies, "I'd love one."

As she passes by him to lead the way upstairs, her perfume lingers and instantly intoxicates him. While mentioning to Alex some of her ideas on decorating the house, Alex struggles to focus on the conversation at hand for being distracted by her slender form and the droplets falling from her hair streaming down the small of her back.

Imagining the sight of her stepping from the shower, her naked body glistening with water; attempting to visualize each curve of her body, as he just about stumbles over the last step, shaking him back to the sound of her voice.

He remarks, "I think you have great ideas for the place. Do you intend to have a decorator take charge of the work or handle it yourself?"

She looks back at him, "Oh, unfortunately these are just ideas. I can't actual put them into effect. My husband says we aren't here enough to put any real detail into the décor; since it is a vacation home."

Alex wants to comment, yet he senses from his better judgment that he should leave well enough alone. Walking into the master bedroom, looking at the large and spacious room with a king-sized wooden canopy bed dressed with sheer white drapes. All of the furniture is entirely of dark cherry from the bed, dresser, two nightstands and even the rocker near the patio door. The floors are polished hard wood. The dark furniture is offset by an all white interior, from the walls to the bedding and drapes.

She leads him out a side entrance off the bedroom, "This is my favorite part of the property." Walking into the tree house style screened in second story room; surrounded on one side by lush trees and flower gardens. Underneath, on the lower level is a large hammock hung from the sturdy beams.

The tree house room, with a large and cozy full sized bed near the large windows, offers a picturesque view of the sea. Alex marvels over the perfect setting inside, from the cabin like interior to the contemporary comforts of the small bar at the back of the room, near a small bathroom. Taylor details the room, "I've been staying out here a great deal. I've found I can't stay inside much. It's too nice out here."

Walking towards her, he states, "It is truly beautiful. I'm sure I'd stay out here myself. This is a fascinating place, much more interesting than mine, I might add."

A smile falters from her face, "This house doesn't have a homely feel to it and I doubt it ever will, no matter what articles it possesses. It has no personality of its own, as yours does."

Noticing a quaint tan wicker rocker loveseat positioned on the opposite side of the bed, facing the direction of the water, Alex motions towards it, "May we sit for awhile and enjoy the view?"

Her face lights up at his suggestion, "That's a great idea."

The two sit side by side, gently rocking in unison, enjoying each other's company on a beautiful afternoon with a mild breeze moving in from the water caressing their skin delicately. Opening a bottle of wine, the two tap their glasses together as they get comfortable and look out at the beautiful view before them.

Taylor ponders the question a moment before turning to Alex, "Do you plan to have a large family?" The question takes Alex a bit off guard while a glimpse enters his mind of what it possibly might be like to be married to Taylor with a family of their own.

The thought warms his heart and causes him to smile, "Yes, hopefully it'll be in the cards for me. I'm not certain on the number. For me, I feel as though I've done the bachelor thing long enough. I'm quite ready to be responsible for someone other than myself. Over time, my priorities have shifted; yet I'm a long way off from having a family. Finding the right person to settle down with is the first step. How about you and your husband? Are there future plans?"

She shifts her position, looking out at the water, "I don't know. I use to think everything would happen on its own in a perfect sequence, but now I'm not certain. I would love to be a mother, I know it would add a fulfilling element in my life; but I know my husband isn't in the same place. He has his career which demands a great deal of his time and focus. I guess it is possible to not be in the cards for us."

Alex smiles while feeling a sense of sorrow. He can see in her eyes that she longs to be happy and from what he has managed to gather about her husband, he believes him to be career oriented, a self involved person who takes his wife for granted; missing out on all the wondrous little details that make her who she is.

Taylor quickly changes the subject before Alex is able to make any further remarks or comments, "Alex, tell me your life's story." He chuckles at the idea of giving her a rundown of his life's story, which he believes wouldn't take longer than 30 minutes to detail.

He begins, "Well, my mum's name is Juliet and my father's name was Phillip. He died when I was seventeen. He ran the family business; acquiring large businesses and implementing restructure. He made many large investments, which continue to bring in large financial profits. I admired my father but I have never aspired to be like him. He worked all the time and made little time for anything or anyone else. I use to wonder if the decision to put business ahead of everything else was ever a regret for him. I know he loved what he did, it drove him. I just know I don't want to be that same type of person."

She feels compassion, listening intently as he continues, "My mum never made a stink over it. I guess she knew when she married him, who he was and what made him tick, so she found her joy in having a son, whom she applied all her focus and attention on. In school, I wasn't a popular kid, not in boarding school or college. I had friends, but I wasn't popular by any means. I worked hard in an attempt to prove myself to my father. I so desperately wanted to gain his approval and love. Unfortunately, he died before I was able to prove what feats and accomplishments I was capable of or the person I would one day become."

Looking out at the water, he feels a moment of weakness in discussing his father; he takes a momentary breath before continuing, "After graduation, I was steadily groomed to take the reigns of my father's company. I have a fabulous partner, Cameron Ryder, who is my right hand man. He steps in if I need a break or aides me in handling various deals at once."

Taylor asks, "Does your mom live in London?"

Taking a small drink from his wine glass he continues, "Yes, she is in London. We are very close. I speak with her every day. She would fall instantly in love with you and agree with delight of you being the idealistic female persuasion for me."

Taylor smiles and with a quizzical brow, inquires, "How so exactly?"

Alex fumbles for the correct wording, "My mum has always insisted that I'm drawn towards the inappropriate type of female. She gathers I lack the ability to distinguish exactly when I'm conversing with the wrong type of female, and for that, I've made a few bad calls with girls I make friends with or otherwise."

She looks at him with a gleam in her eye and a slight devious smile and asks, "May I inquire as to what types of qualities these particular ladies retain?"

With a grin, he knows he has painted himself into a corner with her line of questioning, he proceeds, "Please don't think too badly of me when I confess I tend to go for the attractive and shapely types without making any attempts to discover whether or not they possess any capabilities of carrying on intelligent conversation. Unfortunately, I have been quite shallow in the past, focusing on specific attributes."

A disagreeable expression comes over Taylor's face, not flattered by his reflection of women. All too often is it the case that men look for the allure of the opposite sex, not for what qualities lie within. She knew it too well witnessing first hand her own husband's wandering eyes for the large breasted, model types.

Taylor always believed true beauty in any individual rests from within, giving off the greatest attraction directly from ones soul. Before realizing her harsh reply, the words jump right from her tongue, "May I ask which category I fit, the dimwitted attractive or the unattractive conservationist?"

Quickly, Alex attempts to reverse his misinterpreted depiction, with his rebuttal, "Please, I did not mean for it to come across in such a poor reflection. It is I who has made lapse in judgments in my past, just as I admit I did with you when we first met. I made the assumption that because you are so beautiful that you had that going for you but the first moment you spoke, I knew instantly you were more than a beautiful woman. You are perfect in so many ways. I've never met anyone as divine as you are."

Taylor smiles as she lifts the wine bottle, refreshing Alex's glass. He stops her after she pours half a glass, stating; "Just a little. I'll have to be able to drive home."

She giggles at the remembrance of her inability to hold her alcohol while at Alex's house, "That reminds me for I did not do well on our first meeting. I embarrassed myself greatly. I was hoping to make a nice impression and instead made a fool of myself," says Taylor.

He shakes his head no, "You were stunning and in no way foolish." He studies her ever so intently as she becomes more comfortable, sitting closer and occasionally subtly touching his arm or leg while talking. Every little thing about her seems so in depth and monumental. His heart aches to be more than a friend; feeling regret and disappointment at the acknowledgment she belongs to another.

As the day races away and the night comes on with little warning, the two sit huddled up together gazing out at the warm, glowing sunset as it touches down on the water. Alex asks warmly, "What advice can you offer me on marriage?"

A long pause lingers before a reply is heard, in a quiet voice she replies, "I don't know if I'm the right person to ask for advice on the subject."

In a matter of fact tone, he states, "A marriage should consist of compromise and working towards common goals, not to rationalize one persons goals and dreams are greater to that of the other."

She smiles, unable to hide the sadness in her eyes she quickly looks away, saying "I didn't enter my marriage thinking it would come down to this or ever be like this. I have contemplated the whole thing over and over again to no avail. Sadly, we are not the couple we once were. In the beginning, we felt nothing but love for one another. Over time, I lost sight of myself while standing on the sidelines observing my husband's career take off just as he lost sight of me and the promises he made. I do love my husband, but he is no longer the man I married, nor am I the person I should have been."

Alex suddenly feels his heart sink inside his chest. With all his might he longed to have the ability to make everything perfect for her, make all of her dreams a reality. Supportively he insists, "Taylor, it doesn't have to be this way. You can be whomever you want to be and do as your heart desires, you shouldn't give up on yourself so easily."

She turns on her side, draping her left arm across Alex's chest feeling vulnerable and insecure, "Alex, I wish it were that simple. I have little hopes of my marriage turning around or the idea of my life developing as I had hoped it would years ago. I so enjoy your company and spending time together, I don't want to dampen it with unpleasant conversation."

As Alex runs his left hand across her hair, he gently kisses her forehead. They stay in each other's embrace; relaxed and content, feeling as though being in each other's arms was a safe haven. Not another word is spoken as they now need no further communication to validate the mood.

Awhile later, Alex realizes Taylor has fallen asleep in his arms. With tenderness and a gentle motion, he carefully lifts her up in his strong and sturdy arms, carrying her to the master bedroom, placing her on the bed and covering her gently.

She stirs momentarily when placed on the bed and then settles back into her quiet slumber. Crouched down beside her, watching closely as he touches the soft skin of her face, he whispers, "Taylor Reed, you are precious to me. I must confess my heart beats wildly for you. I never imagined someone like you in it and now I can't imagine my life without you in it. I am doomed to know I've discovered a wondrous thing that cannot be contained. Good night, sweet dreams."

He walks to the doorway, looking back at Taylor as though it could be for the last time. His mind races with conflict as he leaves the house and drives home. With every second he spends with her, he discovers with more and more certainty of how much he adores her and is left wanting more; whether it is one more smile, laugh, touch or look. Reasoning he should cut his ties now before it is too much to bear, he knows deep down he can't bring himself to end it.

CHAPTER 9

UNCHARTERED WATER

T HE FOLLOWING afternoon; the humidity soars as the sun blazes across the sand. Although the air moves gradually providing a continuous breeze, it does little to alleviate the oven-like temperature.

Taylor packs a picnic basket lunch, consisting of chicken, potato salad, homemade rolls and apple pie; an American-style picnic lunch. She carefully goes through each thing she needs to have before leaving; making certain not to leave anything behind.

Smiling, she whisks up the basket, bottle of wine, her purse and her large shady red hat to shield her from the sun's powerful glow. Looking elegant in her red sundress which hugs tightly against her breasts and waist as it flows outward at the skirt, and topped off with her red laced sandals; she gets into her car, driving to Alex's house anxious to surprise him.

The short distance drive finds her peaceful and full of exuberance as she happily sings along with a familiar song playing on the radio. Once at the front door, she quickly rings the doorbell as she struggles with the articles weighing down both hands.

Alex doesn't answer the door. She rings the doorbell once more and with each passing moment the excitement and happy demeanor slowly begins to drift away. Suddenly, she notices the garage door begins to open, as Alex's car pulls slowly out of the driveway.

He stops at the sight of her car blocking his way, looking in the rearview mirror; he sees her standing behind his car. He looks out his open car door window, smiling at her, "Hey, I was just on my way over to your place. I'm going down to the harbor and I was going to see if you'd like to come along for a sail. It's a perfect day for it."

Her face lights up, with the knowledge he truly didn't even have to ask if she'd be interested, for the answer would have been yes with all certainty. Spending time with him would be enjoyable no matter where the location or event. Without hesitation, she agrees and in no time the two stroll off as Alex drives to the docks where his sailboat, Aphrodite, is docked.

Approaching the ship, she reads the name from the large letters displayed on the back of the boat; she remarks, "You named your ship after the Greek goddess of love?"

Her knowledge at knowing the meaning takes Alex by surprise, "Yes, however, she wasn't just the goddess of love but also fertility as well. She was a protectress of sailors. Paris of Troy judged her to be the most beautiful over Hera and Athena. It is said that she saved Paris's life during battle. She was a noble god and this boat is a noble vessel."

Looking at it admiringly, she says, "I love your enthusiasm for Greek mythology. Your boat has a very strong and powerful name. I believe it suits her very well. Am I wrong in assuming it to be female?"

He takes her hand helping her aboard, "Oh, no you're correct. A man's boat is his maiden at sea."

As Taylor gets situated on deck of the lavish sailboat, Alex makes preparations to pull away from the dock. She watches studiously as he mans the boat, steering it away from the bay into the vast open sea. The sun beats down brightly without a cloud visible in sight.

Strong forceful winds gust into the sails, pushing it across the rippling water. He gazes over his shoulder, looking at Taylor as she gazes out at the beautiful scenery taking in all of its brilliance and beauty. Alex remains in awe over her beauty and poise. With little to no effort she captivates him with every pose, movement, smile, speech.

Her hair full and thick, flowing out with the breeze as her dress playfully dances farther up her leg as the air pushes underneath the skirt of her dress. With all his might, he forces himself to look away, fearful she might catch him staring at her.

Just as he thinks he got away with the crime, Taylor catches a glimpse of him looking, which brings a quick smile to her face. Carefully, she stands feeling as though her sea legs aren't going to willingly carry her across the rocky deck over to him. With a quick and steady motion, she pushes herself towards him, latching onto his waist; holding to him tightly.

Grasping one hand over hers, he assures her, "I won't let you fall. You're safe here with me. Would you like to steer for a bit?" She looks petrified at the suggestion. He laughs, "It will be okay, I promise, you won't be here by yourself."

The idea scares her tremendously, "Alex, I don't know how to steer a boat. I really shouldn't."

Moving around her in a move so debonair and quick as if on a dance floor; he stands behind her, close against her body, holding his mouth close to her ear; "You can do it, and there isn't much to it really. It is a good deal like driving a car or riding a bike except with less traffic. There aren't other boats close by, so all you need is a few slight adjustments in steering."

He stands behind her for a few minutes as she gains confidence in herself manning the helm. As they get further out to sea, Alex presses one arm firmly around her waist, while pointing out different land marks as they pass by.

After a bit, Alex drops the sails and anchor in a beautiful secluded bay to the south. They go below deck and sit side by side at the dinette table, enjoying the picnic lunch, laughing and joking with each other.

Taylor remarks, "I could easily live at sea. It is so peaceful and beautiful. No city traffic or endless counts of people. No troubles or cares—I could easily get use to this."

He replies with a proud and bold manner, joking, "That's it then. It is decided, we'll never return to shore."

In her heart, she wishes it could be a realistic promise, yet she knows it isn't possible. In such a short time, she has grown quite fond of Alex; wishing the situation was different and they could be more than friends. If only their paths could have crossed sooner; their lives would be so altered.

The day seems to just fly by as they enjoy their time together in the bay. In late afternoon, with the sun moving off in the distance; they sit on deck, Taylor resting her back against Alex's chest; as he holds her close, she holds onto his bracing arms as they hold fastening across her chest.

No words are uttered for their hearts have begun speaking a language of their own; feeling the exact same emotions, longing and desiring to be together; unclouded by the opposition. As their minds struggle to give reassurance to the multitudes of reasons they could not fall in love or be together, their hearts argued to overturn the sternness of their mind's ruling.

By no means was it a loss to Taylor in the realization of what she had to lose if she were to act on impulse. She was in fact married, whereas Alex was not. She considered the consequences she would face if she allowed things to escalate only to be discovered. There was no question, Jonathan would without question kill her and likely Alex as well.

Many times, often in a heated argument, Jonathan vowed he would never lose her or let her go; giving the solemn promise that she would be dead before he'd allow either to happen. He meant every word. The thought drifted in her mind, wondering to herself if it be worth the risk. Her heart answered quickly, yes; however, she knew she couldn't think such things or allow herself to feel this way.

She moves on her side, still warmly held in Alex's embrace, as she looks up at him. He smiles, wondering what thoughts plague her; wishing she shared thoughts similar to his own. He desperately wanted nothing more than to take hold of her and kiss her passionately with every fiber of his being and beat of his heart.

Moments later as he looks deeply into her eyes, he makes the decision to break the silence as he knows the sun is shifting, getting closer to setting, "We should head back towards the harbor; it will be dark in a few hours. I doubt you'd want to be out here spending the night. There will be little light to guide us back," says Alex.

Unbeknownst to Taylor, she sits up with a newfound clarity and determination; sensing a calm she cannot describe, she utters words she distinctively knows she has no desire to take back; she asks "Could we stay? I don't want to go back."

Immediately, Alex's heart sinks inside his chest as his adrenalin begins to race quickly through his veins, "Are you certain?"

The wind blows through her hair, "Yes, more certain than I've ever been. I want to be with you. I don't want to question anything. All I want is you, to be right here with you," says Taylor.

His face lights up with joy and sheer exhilaration, uncertain if he is dreaming or if the dream has miraculously just come true. He takes no time to question or reason anything; just knowing she too wants to be with him is all he needs to know.

As the sun glistens behind her, providing a luminous outline as she gazes longingly into Alex's warm brown eyes, he gently holds her face within his hands; slowly moving forward, looking deeply within her eyes; kissing her with an unbridled passion he has held captive.

His kiss reverberates with warmth and passion, evoking stronger feelings from within them both. Lost in his eyes, Taylor feels weak in the knees; leaning in closer, feeling his sweet breathe against her cheek.

Standing up, he extends his hand to Taylor. Taking her hand in his, he takes her below deck carefully lowering her down on the bed as his arm anchors her. As she lies across the bed, her eyes never leave his, watching as he removes his shirt; crawling onto the bed, hovering over her as his muscles tighten as he supports his weight on top of her body.

Taylor marvels in every detail of his form, running her fingers up his firm and contoured arms all the way up to his dark wavy hair. Running her hands up his back, she feels the toned muscles of his shoulders and forearms, as they are actively pulsating.

As he lowers, applying his body weight on top of her she feels a sense of urgency come over her; wanting him stronger than before, ready to devour him like a hungry lion in the African terrain.

His eyes look deeply into hers as if they are under a deep trance. A sense of curiosity and intrigue races through her mind; wondering what he's thinking as he looks at her so intently, in a way no one has ever looked at her before.

With soft, gentle lips, he kisses her playfully, teasing her with each touch of his lips before moving slowly down her neck. Such simple pleasures now become erotic sensations offering intense euphoria. Slowly he moves his right hand along her left leg gently caressing her soft skin, moving higher up to her thigh, causing her breathing to escalate; becoming labored in anxious anticipation.

Taylor pulls her sundress off over her head, revealing her lacey red thong panties and bare breasts. Alex looks admiringly at every beautiful body part, from her belly button, contoured hips to her perfectly proportioned breasts. The vision of her naked body sends a rush of blood racing throughout his body.

Engorged and now anxious himself, he kisses her passionately eager to express himself effortlessly; yet forcing himself to slow the pace down knowing he must savor each moment and make it last as long as possible. This would not be a time to thrust himself forward without making it worthy of focusing on her intently.

As he plans to take it slow, Taylor has different plans of her own. The urgency is too great and teasing in a way she can no longer bear. While in the throws of kissing, she shifts the control from him to her; moving on top of him, kissing him feverishly from his neck all the way down his chest.

She unfastens his pants, pushing them down until they fall from his legs. Releasing him from his pants he now freely becomes erect as she strokes him gently. The sensation of her soft hand firmly set in motion leaves him submissive and vulnerable as he grabs hold of the sheets tightly, in an attempt to stifle his escalating pleasure from each inflicted stroke of movement.

Quickly he knows he must turn the tables or it will be too much for him to withstand. Flipping her back down on the bed, he presses down on her. She feels his girth pressing between her legs as he kisses her with unbridled desire.

Anxiously, she says in a labored breath, "Alex, I want you now." Attempting to pull her delicate panties down, he grips too tightly and in one brisk and sudden move, rips them off; causing her to become more aroused by the wildness in his demeanor.

As the night smothers out any remaining rays of light from the sun, Alex and Taylor enjoy the rapture of lovemaking, oblivious to anything other than each other as they tirelessly pursue every outlet of pleasuring the other.

During a role reversal as Taylor towers over top, her energy lessens as she begins to tire; sweat dripping from her dangling hair while beads of sweat race down to the small of her back. Carefully Alex holds close to her body and with a delicate and swift motion, he flips her underneath his body as he begins to set things back in motion, offering very little pause.

The temperature quickly rises as their sweaty bodies begin to slide against each other, their hair ringing wet, with the droplets of sweat from his hair piercing her skin like a gentle rainstorm. Between them there is a force of passion bigger and more powerful than the both of them.

Shaken by the intensity, she surprises herself with a collective outcry as she feels the pressure between her legs; heighten to a plateau she can no longer withstand. As they lay naked, nuzzling close together breathing deeply as if attempting to breath for the first time; Taylor finds herself mesmerized by Alex's lovemaking.

Their passion is an awakening of an unquenchable thirst; one of an unstoppable presence. As they make love up until the early hours of the morning, they finally collapse in each other's arms due to sheer exhaustion.

As the morning dawns on a new day, shining bright rays of light into the cabin, warming their naked bodies; Alex sleeps as Taylor lies in his arms with her head resting gently on his chest while her mind races with turmoil and fear.

Suddenly a tear escapes from her eye, streaming down her cheek piercing Alex's chest. He wakes at the touch of the tear as it lands on his skin, immediately looking at her alarmed, "Why are you crying? Did I do something to hurt you?"

Sitting up, she puts on a smile and gently caresses the left side of his face, professing, "No, everything you did was magnificent and terrific. I've never been as happy as I am right now. I want to hold on to this for as long as possible. My tears are tears of joy and happiness, I assure you." He moves in closer, kissing her with a warm, loving kiss.

As they set out to return to the harbor, Taylor holds closely to Alex's chest from behind, resting her head against his back. Without any warning, he swings her around swiftly to face him, with her back pressed against the helm. He looks into her eyes with passion and expressive desire, with a soft sensual tone he professes, "I would love nothing more than to tie you to the helm and make love to you as we make our way to shore."

Still a bit shaken by his sudden action, she wonders if he is serious and then questions in her mind if it would even be physically possible. Before she has an opportunity to contemplate the scenario, he begins to kiss her passionately, pressing her body tightly against his waist. Feeling the virile and protruding force against her body, she too becomes driven and aroused, unable to think of anything else.

With nothing but the open air and sea surrounding them for miles, Taylor feels no holds of shame or intimidation. For once in her life she has a completely different outlook on her sexuality and self expression, dropping her guard; allowing things to happen as they may.

She eagerly pulls Alex's shirt over his head before fervently unfastening his shorts. He doesn't utter a word as he solely focuses in on her eyes as they gaze up at him attentively; as she lifts her dress above her hips, exposing her nakedness to his admiring gaze. The adrenaline rush races throughout her body, causing her heart to beat in a rapid rhythm.

Her warm, pink lips kiss gently down his neck as the direction turns south down his chest, inching closer and closer towards his waist; while his muscles pulsate with each delicate touch of her lips and stroke of her soft hands. With a gentle hand, she graciously pushes his shorts down, stroking his manhood with a slow, steady pace. His eyes close as each movement tortures him; all the while he patiently waits the moment he can take her in his arms and ravish her with all the passion she drives from within him.

Unable to withstand any further temptation, he carefully hoists her against the large wooden wheel, making his way ever so gently between the curves of her inner thighs. Their bodies rock against each other, just as the vessel crashes against the shifting waves with the wind pressing sternly into the sails carrying it across the open sea.

Nervously, Alex begins to fear not only losing control of himself but also of manning the boat. Unable to shift his attention to anything other than Taylor's gentle and erotic touch, as she kisses his neck passionately all the while eagerly she manually pulls his body closer and harder towards her own.

In the throws of the hot sun, wind, and sea; they become one in their own storm of passion in which nothing can halter. Alex makes love to her with so much force and gusto, yet does it so in a delicate manner, careful not to hurt her. His arms grip ever so tightly around her holding her up, as he struggles to grip the large wooden wheel, doing his best to keep the boat on course.

As the waves and wind forcefully press against the sails; the ship lunges forward as they no longer share focus on their surroundings, for they are now lost in each other. She remains fixated on his eyes as he looks at her with an indescribable stare. The only way she could compare it would be a cross between a look of being mesmerized and perhaps enchantment.

Later as they pull into the harbor; a fellow sailor aides Alex in tying the ship to the dock and as they begin walking back towards the car, Alex wraps his arm around her waist, "I'm afraid we mustn't make love on the ship again while it is in motion, for I lost direction and we had to back-track for a long distance just to get back to the harbor."

She smiles as she reflects on the enthralling passion they shared as they made love on deck, in such a tight hold of each other; testing the risks and elements. The danger offered such a thrilling enticement unlike anything she had ever experienced before and possibly ever would.

CHAPTER 10

DIFFICULT DECISIONS

L ATER THAT evening, back at Alex's house, the two kick off their shoes and curl up on the sofa in front of the fireplace as a small fire burns. Alex wastes no time, eagerly clutching onto Taylor; kissing her passionately, hovering overtop of her as he swiftly lowers his body on top of her.

One kiss is all it takes, all that is needed to cause him to want more of her. The addiction to her is so great and powerful. She wraps her arms around his neck, feeling her heart race as the passion erupts from within.

His mesmerizing brown eyes gaze at her lovingly, placing her in an ever so arousing hypnotic trance. As a playful smile dances across his face, like a child who has just discovered a valuable secret and without any warning or a word uttered, he gets up whisking her into his arms and over his shoulder, carrying her through the house to the master bedroom. Feeling as though she were Jane in a Tarzan film, she inquires, "Alex, where are you taking me?" He doesn't utter a word.

To her surprise, he passes the bed and places her down inside the large and extravagant master bathroom. Beige marble tiles cover the walls and shower, while on the adjacent side full length mirrors surround the sink and countertop. A large skylight hangs in a high portion of the ceiling. It is unlike anything she has seen before with its overwhelming size and openness.

Alex turns the dual showerheads on in the walk in shower with its three clear glass doors. In no time, the steam builds fogging up the entire room. He gently touches a side of her face, "I adore everything about you." He holds a section of her dress skirt in his hand, looking at her seductively, "May I?"

She could feel the words lodged in her throat, unable to escape; reluctantly she manages to nod her head yes in agreement. Alex slowly and carefully undresses her, not once taking his eyes away from hers;

moving in close to kiss her soft, wet lips. With his breath labored, expanding in unison with hers; she pulls at his shirt, anxious to remove it in order to feel his warm skin pressed against her own.

As he removes his shorts and pulls her body against his, she begins to feel weak in the knees as she hears the deep pounding of her heart within her own chest. He smiles at her reassuringly, sensing her insecurity by the unsettled gaze of her eyes.

Standing together naked in the dimly lit bathroom, with little effort, he lifts her up taking a few steps forward into the shower. The warm water runs down her face and hair, trickling down. Closing her eyes taking in the sensation of the water, she begins to notice it less and less as his hands explore the many depths of her body.

He magically sends her to a euphoric place never before traveled or explored. Looking in his eyes as they are fixated upon hers; they tell more than any eyes she has ever seen; through them, it is a mirror into his soul, reflecting passion, lust, sincerity, and a love unlike any other. In that moment she realizes on all three occasions of love making, his eyes reflected a different look from any casual look given; far more pronounced. She loses herself within them.

With little interruption, the experience goes from the shower to the bedroom. The large scale bedroom flourishes with a dark décor, consisting of maroon satin sheets and a black satin bedspread. The large windows start at the floor and go all the way up to the tall ceiling, draped with long flowing maroon curtains.

Matching sheer satin drapes cover the canopy of the massive dark cherry poster bed. The moonlight from right outside the large windows gently illuminates the inside of the room. No thoughts of food has entered their minds while twenty-four hours later all that now sustains them is the hunger they share for each other; a hunger that cannot be fulfilled or satisfied.

The moon's light moves across the night's sky, leaving the room in deepened darkness. Sight becomes a lost sense; all the while the sense of touch is awakened. Their naked bodies lie in the bed, pressed against each other, supplying intense body heat.

In a rhythmic motion, steadily moving back and fourth; she holds tightly to his sweaty body, gasping for heated air as the body heat between them becomes hotter. As his chest comes in contact with her wet breasts, she feels the pounding of his heart as each labored breath strikes her skin.

After several hours of prolonged lovemaking, Alex drifts off to sleep while Taylor listens in the dark as his breathing becomes calm while in a restful sleep. She herself is unable to rest or sleep for too many things are racing through her mind. Her new found love for Alex and the reality of her situation, she is a married woman. Questions replay over and over that she is unable to offer an answer to.

The questions loom; she wonders if she has made a terrible mistake. How could the triangle of three go along without someone getting hurt in the process? As she longs to relish the time she has with Alex, she struggles to push the pressing thoughts of despair from her mind, at least until morning when she can look upon things rationally.

Wearily, she falls to sleep in Alex's arms where she has a spectacular dream, envisioning herself in a life with Alex; living in a beautiful home with children, a career, and a life of never ending happiness. The dream is so vivid it feels so real that briefly once she wakes, she believes it to be true.

She carefully lies still, watching Alex as he sleeps. The early morning sun barely filters through the windows as dawn slowly approaches. The urgency presses her to get up and leave as she knows she can't bring herself to face him and break off their relationship. Hurting him is the last thing she wants to have happen.

Gently she pulls out from underneath his warm embrace and off the bed; watching him the entire time for fear that he'll open his eyes to witness her leaving. She quickly retrieves her clothes and dresses, listening intently for sounds of him stirring. Her heart aches as the tears begin to well up in her eyes.

In one last adoring moment, she stands quietly at the foot of the bed, watching as he sleeps. A tear streams down her cheek as a sharp stabbing pain in her heart closely cripples her where she stands. She unwillingly leaves before giving into the desire to crawl back into bed, never to leave his side.

On the drive home, all of her emotions come crashing together; causing her to cry uncontrollably. She knew she wouldn't regret the time spent with Alex, yet she had no inclination on just how profound severing ties with him could be. It was apparent just how much she now cares for him and nothing would change the way she feels.

A short time later, Alex stirs and wakens in his bed, alone. Reaching his arm out to cradle Taylor, he finds she isn't where he had expected her to be. Happily he rises grabbing his bath robe from a chair, wrapping his naked form; as he joyfully makes his way through the house in search of Taylor, searching and calling out her name room by room.

He soon discovers she isn't in the house as his calls go unanswered. Thoughts begin to race through his mind, wondering why she would up and leave without saying good-bye. He began to ponder the thought further, wondering if he had in fact done something to drive her away, unknowingly.

At the same time back at the villa, Taylor stares off in a blank stare as she feels ultimately torn and detached, for she wants nothing more than to be with Alex, yet she is resolved in the knowledge she cannot walk out on her husband or their marriage. Her reasoning and perspective assures her she must end the affair now.

Steadily she begins to calm herself, easing her grief. Glancing at the phone debating whether or not to call Alex; after all it wasn't in her character to be rude and leave without saying good-bye. She notices the answering machine's message light flashing.

She hesitates at listening to the message; however she is anxious to hear Alex's voice. She presses the play button, to hear the angry voice of her husband, "Taylor, why aren't you answering the phone?!" The second message plays with even more hostility in his voice, "Taylor, I don't like this. You have no reason to be ignoring my calls." The third and final message rants, "Taylor this is enough! I have called you repeatedly. Call me immediately!"

Wiping the tears from her face, she picks up the receiver and takes a deep breath as she calls Jonathan. He goes right into interrogating her, "Where have you been? I've called you repeatedly, what is going on?!"

Her voice falters as she begins to speak, "Jonathan, I'm sorry. I've had a horrible headache. One of my migraines; which I haven't had in a long time. I ended up getting sick and I went to bed. I apologize for not answering and causing you to worry."

Jonathan pauses briefly before responding in a mellow manner, "I'm sorry. Are you feeling better?"

She replies, "Yes. I believe I spent too much time in the sun and heat."

Jonathan continues, "Taylor, I wanted you to get out and enjoy yourself, not overdo it; stay indoors today. I have promising news; my case is going to trial next week, sooner than planned, so as soon as I win the case, I'll join you and we can begin our vacation together. I can't wait to see you. I miss you so much."

Tears fall from Taylor's eyes, "I've missed you too," says Taylor.

"I have to go babe. I'll call you later to see how you're doing. I love you." "I love you too." Collapsing to the couch, her sadness rises again from within, as she feels her life unraveling beyond her control. Guilt plagues her as the revelation emerges she doesn't wish to see her husband or be reunited with him.

Before meeting Alex, her life consisted of monotonous repetition and unwavering negativity; now, everything was different and her life showed meaning and purpose. She knew she also longed for Alex and the way he makes her feel, the way her heart would beat wildly along with the passion she felt at the pure sight of him.

Suddenly, Taylor hears a frantic knock at the front door. Her heart pounds rapidly at the thought of seeing Alex and then an earth shattering nervousness takes hold, making her weary of opening the door. She reaches for the door, knowing the outcome that she faces.

Alex stands before her, confused and uncertain of what events have altered and led to her standing before him with tears in her eyes. He pleads, "What have I done? Please tell me what I did wrong."

She wipes her eyes taking a deep breath, "You did nothing wrong. Please don't think that way; I left because I couldn't face you to tell you good bye, just as it pains me at this very moment."

Unable to grasp why she is saying these things, he asks, "Why would you have to say good-bye?"

She struggles to fight off the tears, "Alex, I'm married. I cannot lead you on thinking we could have something more or any normalcy even, when the fact is this could only be a short lived romance. It wouldn't be fair to you. We must put an end to this before it becomes impossible to part."

He gently grabs hold of her arms, looking her in the eyes with a compassionate glance, "I know you're married and it honestly breaks my heart, for I would love nothing more than to claim you as my own love. This thought has raced through my mind ever since you made mention of you being married. My heart speaks for me while my conscience states reprimand for the way of my heart. I cannot ask you to aid in my wanting heart's desires, but to remain my friend, for I cannot lose you entirely. Please don't turn me away," pleads Alex.

Taylor throws herself into Alex's arms, holding onto him tightly as she mentally faces her dilemma. "Alex, I want you in the same way. I have fallen in love with you. My heart aches to be with you and to be apart causes me the greatest pain I've ever had to endure. I don't want to be apart from you; however, I don't see how delaying the inevitable will offer us any solace."

He holds tightly to her, fearing if he lets go he'll never see her again. He gently pulls away, holding her face in the palms of his hands as he bends in closely looking deeply into her eyes, he says "I love you, Taylor, and even though this is a forbidden love we share; I know deep down in my heart that I was meant to find you and experience the wonders of true love. Yes, we will have to be contented with the time that is allotted us, but let us not deny ourselves the valuable time we still have before us."

Seeing the longing in his eyes and knowing he too cannot bear to part, she agrees with him and together they make a pact to savor what time they have left, whether it is an hour, day, week or month and agree to part when the time comes. Their hearts; however greedy, yearn to be together and to never be parted.

Alex smiles tenderly at Taylor; as he kisses her gently, running his fingers through her flowing hair, "I have a few things to attend to and then I'll return and we'll have dinner. I won't be long. I promise. I want to see you smile again. Never do I wish to see tears fall from your pretty eyes."

She smiles, even though inside the knowledge that the affair will be short lived drowns her spirits. He kisses her again and reluctantly pulls away, glancing back several times as he walks away from her, as though he fears she will disappear if his glance is off her too long.

As the afternoon passes and evening draws closer, Taylor gets ready for Alex's return sitting in a lounge chair on the back porch watching as the sun sets, reflecting on the circumstances of the day. Jonathan calls briefly to check on her and after the call, she takes notice that had she cared enough about the state of her marriage and had it still been dear to her as it once was, she would not be forsaking it or her heart.

There wasn't a doubt in her mind that she didn't still in fact care deeply for Jonathan, but it wasn't the same. He had placed more importance and emphasis on his career instead of his marriage and not being allowed to have a career of her own, caused disenchantment and instability within herself.

Alex returns a short time later to pick up Taylor, dressed dashingly in a suit and tie with a large bouquet of long stem red roses. She smiles and her heart beats wildly at his presence. Dinner could easily be skipped if she could just rest within his arms and kiss his lips into the night.

He studies her, admiring her beauty in a flowing black dress with dark red lace trim and a matching red lace shawl draped across her shoulders. "You look lovely. These are for you. I want to have you smiling again. Too many tears were lost." She smiles at him.

As he looks at her, Alex finds it hurts just to gaze upon her, all the while wanting to have her as his own, wife, lover, spouse. For so long he had hoped to find his soul mate, one who could make him think of nothing else, to compliment him in a way no one or anything else could. Here he has found it that which he seeks in the one person he'll never have claim of.

Glancing at his watch, "I made reservations at a restaurant called Castaway. It's a small family owned place just on the outskirts of town." She smiles at him, "It sounds lovely."

During the thirty minute drive few words are spoken. Alex's hand searches for Taylor's. She takes his hand as words don't have to be spoken for their hearts are able to speak volumes. They arrive at the quaint little restaurant that has only one car parked in its lot.

White twinkle Christmas lights dangle from the overhang. Even though it isn't Christmas, it offers a nice touch to the building. Inside, small tables are spaced out, covered with red tablecloths and candle centerpieces. A heavy set older Italian man walks towards them. He welcomes them with a jolly laugh, "Hello, Alex! It has been too long my friend. How have you been?"

Alex smiles, "Angelo, I'm doing well. How's the family?"

The man lights up with joy, "The family couldn't be better. Since you were last here, I've had an addition to the family, a girl. Her name is Katarina."

Alex replies, "Congratulations! So, she is your seventh, right?"

The old man boosts, "Yes, with the eighth on the way."

Angelo glances over at Taylor who stands quietly beside Alex, "And who is this lovely young lady next to you?"

Alex turns to Taylor, "Angelo, this is Taylor Reed."

The short cheery man glances at Alex and back to Taylor, as he takes her hand in his, "I can tell she is very special. Taylor, you are a beautiful woman. I have known Alex for several years. He comes to my restaurant every time he's on the island. The entire time I've known him, he has not once brought a date along. I cannot tell you how pleased I am to see he has found someone special to share his life with. I knew it would happen and once it did that he'd find happiness forever. I'm certain the two of you will be very happy together."

Taylor smiles, looking softly at Alex; "He makes me happier than I ever imagined possible. I know he's a true treasure." She speaks from her heart yet it pains her greatly to know what they share briefly will be short-lived. At the same moment, Alex too feels saddened reading the message in her eyes. The inevitable makes each moment that much more precious.

Angelo seats the couple at a small quaint table near a large window, "I will make you both a wonderful dinner. I will cook it myself, which I only do on special occasions. Back home in Italy, my late mother was marveled as the best cook in our small village. Her dishes were made with love and happiness, all who ate her cooking would become filled with those very emotions. I can cook like my mother and blessed your dinner will be. I will bring you a bottle of wine and begin preparing your dinner."

As they enjoy the wine, passing flirty glances to one another, Taylor rests her chin on the palm of her upturned hand, looking at Alex, "Angelo is very nice and I can see why this is such a special place."

With a smile, Alex remarks to her, "Just don't go falling in love with him. I know I'm no Angelo, but I adore you beyond imagination. I would hate to see him win out over me."

She giggles, "That isn't possible."

Alex continues, "You haven't tasted his cooking yet. This is an honor; he doesn't cook for just anyone. He usually has Antonio do all of the cooking." Taylor releases her hand, reaching across the table, touching his hand.

Alex looks at Taylor with gentle eyes and asks, "Would you like to dance?"

She glances around the vacant room, she asks, "Here?"

With a short wink he replies, "Yes."

Gently she nervously bites down on her bottom lip, before shaking her head yes.

As they begin to dance closely, she rests her head against his chest listening to the soft music playing; feeling as safe and content in his arms as she has ever felt anywhere before and doubted would likely again. To remain in this spot for eternity would be a pleasant wish come true.

He speaks in a gentle voice, "Taylor, I love you."

She replies softly, "I love you too."

Awhile later, as Angelo delivers their lasagna he smiles happily at his masterpiece, "I cannot tell you what is in my mother's famous lasagna, but I can tell you, there is no other like it in the world. I'll leave you now to enjoy. Eat up."

They begin dining on their magnificent meal. Alex notices Taylor sizing up the plate of food, "You don't have to eat all of it. That's the Italian way, plenty of good food. I couldn't do it at first either and believe me; a nice jog is in store for me tomorrow," says Alex.

Outside a rainstorm rapidly beats against the windows, leaving a pool of water on the road. She watches mesmerized as the rain beats angrily on anything in its path, as she states as a matter of fact, "I've always fantasized of making love in a rainstorm. To feel the cool drops from above as it runs down your body; drenching you from head to toe, all the while held in a close and passionate embrace: In the throws of something unstoppable it would be quite seductive."

Alex can see her vision as though he is already there. Oblivious that Angelo has returned with a tray of desserts and coffee, "May I interest either of you with dessert or coffee?"

Alex struggles to pull himself away from the hypnotic state he has fallen victim to, "No, thank you, Angelo. I'm afraid we must be on our way. Thank you for such a wonderful meal, as always. I promise we'll return soon."

Angelo insists, "Yes, you must. Rosa will be so pleased to hear you're in town. You must come back on a weekend when she is here, so she can meet your lovely lady. I will get your check."

After taking care of the bill, Alex races with Taylor in the downpour to open her car door. Without a word, Alex pulls away from the parking lot with a sense of urgency. She notices his anxiousness fearing something is wrong, she asks "Are we late for something?"

He replies, "I don't intend to be. We're not far."

He drives down an old abandoned road, surrounded by many tall trees. Parking in a desolate area; he turns off the ignition. She looks out her window at the dark wooded landscape, barely able to see much of anything as no moon is visible on this night, "Alex, where are we?"

His face takes on a mischievous smile, "Ever since you told me about your idea in the rain, I can't stop thinking about it, or it with you. I want to make love to you in the rain, right here, right now."

Resting her hand tightly on the door handle, she smiles, "I'll meet you outside."

As she jumps out of the car, she races towards the front. Alex darts out only seconds behind her. As if in a timed contest, both remove their clothes, tossing them on top of the hood. He wraps his arms around her, lifting her up into his unyielding arms as he cautiously braces her against the car.

With her long legs coiled around his waist, the rain splashing rapidly against her bare breasts, as her liquid lips are pressed to Alex's in a passionate lock. The refreshing rain drizzles warmly overtop of them as they begin to lose sight of it, falling deeply into each other.

Their lovemaking begins to steadily slow to a rhythmic pace only to escalate into an intense, energetic force as their bodies become intertwined. To Taylor's amazement, she discovers the reality of the moment offers so much more than she could have ever expected or imagined.

Alex holds onto her carefully and gently in his strong arms, laying her across the hood of the car, as his hands grip her thighs; thrusting himself deeper and deeper inside as she moans with passion. The mood unleashes a wild and driven excitement from within him. Something this special could be shared with her and no other.

Her hands squeeze tightly against his wrists as the intensity sends her to a place of elation. The cool metal of the car sends chills through her body as she struggles to fight against the urge to succumb to climatic pleasure.

In his eyes she senses the moment is close at hand and as the intensity grows and the will to fight it diminishes, together they reach the final plateau; their bodies clinging closely together, savoring every last second of an act of pure splendor.

During the ride home, both drenched and trying to warm up with the heater blowing on them; Taylor begins to laugh helplessly. Alex inquires, "What do you find humorous?"

She looks at him, "Oh, just how no matter where we are or what the condition, I'm finding myself becoming less reserved about my indiscretions. I would be with you anywhere. This is a self-discovery." They both smile at each other.

Back at the villa, candles light the master bedroom with a warm and subtle glow. Alex's arms hold snuggly around Taylor's waist as she sleeps peacefully in his warm embrace. He is unable to sleep for too many thoughts and feelings race through his heart and mind, troubling him immensely.

The irrefutable knowledge that sooner or later her husband will arrive and their romance will end abruptly. Without question he would do anything to make that day not come. She has changed every aspect of his life in such a short time; giving him a taste of something he has never had all the while showing him what happiness is and proving once and for all it does exist.

CHAPTER 11

LETTING GO

I N THE morning, a gentle breeze filters into the room from the open patio doors and windows as a cloudy sky hides the sun. Taylor opens her eyes, expecting to see Alex and instead sees she is in the room alone.

Sitting up in bed attempting to gain her bearings and contemplate her next forward motion, she is hindered by the phone ringing. She answers, "Hello."

The voice of her husband sounds from the other end, "Hi, baby. It's so good to hear your voice. I miss you."

Looking around the room with thoughts racing in her mind, she mechanically says, "Hi, I miss you too."

His voice quaint and adoring, an unfamiliar sound, he continues, "I know from first hand experience, I can never be separated from you like this ever again. I'm lost without you."

As Taylor replies she notices Alex coming quietly around the corner from the hallway hearing each and every word, "I can't wait to see you. When can you leave New York?" Her eyes meet his as she misses what Jonathan says as he tells her it won't be long, with his case being deliberated now.

Her voice falters as she struggles to keep her composure, "Let me know when you're due to arrive and I'll pick you up from the airport."

Jonathan holds his own as the realization of her wish for forewarning makes the deceit even more obvious, "Oh, I'll let you know as soon as I do. Be prepared for the two of us to spend some quality time together. We'll have a lot to make up for, you and me. I'll let you go. I love you."

The displeasing expressing on Alex's face breaks her heart as she tells her husband goodbye. Hurting him is not something she ever intended to do or least of all have happen, yet there is little avoidance of that under the circumstances.

Standing from the bed, as the sheet drops from her body to the floor, exposing her naked form; she walks towards Alex's stern posed body, wrapping her arms around his waist holding tightly to him; "I'm sorry. I wish the circumstances were different and not the situation it happens to be," says Taylor.

Alex's voice replies softly, "It doesn't have to be. This could end so differently where we can both be happy, together."

She looks up at him quizzically, "How could that possibly be?"

He takes her hands in his, speaking with a profound excitement in his voice, "I've done a great deal of thinking about this and it is simple. We leave together and lose ourselves where nobody can trace us. Anywhere you want to go, we'll make a life together. He'll never find us, I promise."

Taylor's eyes drop to the floor as the doubt takes back over, "You don't know Jonathan. He would not stop searching until I was found. I can't put you in harms way. It would be too risky. Believe me, I'd love nothing more than to run off with you and make a life of our own, but no matter how far we ran or how well we thought we covered our tracks, he'd find us and kill us both."

Alex takes a different approach, reassuring her, "I have a close friend who works for the government, he could help us, create a new identity for you, everything. It's not impossible, this will work. All I have to do is place a call and get things started. What do you say?"

Anxiously he hangs on as seconds pass, studying her face intently in hopes she will see his vision and embrace it. Her eyes light up as she begins to smile, "Okay, talk to your friend, and see if he can help us."

Words cannot express the volume of excitement that races from within. He kisses her on the cheek before racing down the hallway. His footsteps stop as the sound becomes closer as he returns, taking her in his arms tightly; kissing her most ardently. He tells her before leaving, "I love you. I'll be back soon."

Returning home, Alex quickly heads straight for the telephone, calling his best friend since childhood, Graham Rosser, back in London. Graham delights in hearing the sound of his friend's voice, "Alex, I was beginning to wonder what happened to you, whether you fell from the face of the earth or just possibly abducted by aliens. I haven't heard from you in ages. What's going on?"

Alex rushes right into detailing his dilemma, "I need your help, Graham. I'm in Australia; I've met the woman I want to spend the rest of my life with. The only problem is she's married."

Graham quickly interjects, "Whoa! Alex, are you sure you know what you're doing? A married woman is going to make nothing but trouble for you."

Alex rallies for Taylor, "If you met her, you would not have to ask such a question. I don't want to lose her."

Graham continues hastily, "Do you realize what you're saying? You don't have her to lose, she's married and you shouldn't be involved in an affair. You're setting yourself up for a major disaster."

Alex sighs sensing his friend isn't going to aid him as easily as he had hoped, "Listen, her husband is an attorney who happens to be in New York right now and he is due to join her out here soon. She is fearful of him and she is willing to leave the island with me before he has time to arrive. I need your help; I need you to pull some strings and get a new identity for her. This needs to happen immediately before it's too late."

Graham pauses briefly, "Alex, do you hear what you're saying?! This is not possible. What you're asking I can't do for you. Changing ones identity is for witness protection purposes, not to steal another man's wife and relocate to start a new life together. You need to cut your ties before something serious takes place, like her husband returning to discover you're messing with his wife and then kill you. This is not characteristic of you at all."

Alex pleads, "I need this from you, please don't fail me. I wouldn't ask this of you if there were any other way. I love her and I just can't lose her. I've never asked you for anything and I realize this is asking a lot, please help me make this happen."

Graham makes one last effort to reach his friend, "Come to your senses; return to London, call Carmen. The two of you were good together and with her you know she is a sure thing."

"I wasn't happy in the past. She makes me happier than I've ever been. I want Taylor. She is the only one for me; I can't see my life without her in it."

Alex hears exasperation in his friend's voice, "I can't make you any promises, Alex. I'll see what I can do, but odds are you're grasping at air. I have someone that owes me a favor. Don't get your hopes up too soon; this favor may be too big to call a return on."

Once Alex hangs up the phone, he smiles at the revelation his plan is set in motion. Nothing is impossible; finding a way to make the getaway happen will take place, one way or another. If Graham doesn't come through, Alex concurs he has the financial means to find someone who can make it happen.

As the day ends and evening approaches, the night air holds a heavy, dry heat. Taylor stands in front of a standing fan letting the air strike against her skin in a failing attempt to find comfort. The idea of sleeping in a pool of water sounds delightful: anything to escape the heat.

Patiently most of her day was spent waiting to hear from Alex, with no sign or word. More and more she found she relied upon him greatly, whether it be companionship, to talk, or held up in his arms. Without him, she discovered herself lost. She had no idea how she'd readjust to him not being around.

Sitting on the sofa, she stretches her bare legs along the couch, lying down with a romance novel prepared to entertain herself for the remainder of the evening. While only a few pages in, a sound comes from the open patio doors. She strains her eyes to see in the darkness what lingers outside. Her heart races as the fear of danger lurks from outside.

She rises slowly, moving hesitantly towards the doors; her heart racing with each step. As she almost makes it to the patio; Alex comes out of nowhere. She lets out a sharp scream as a look of passing fear shows on her face.

Alex stands with flowers in hand, dressed in tan khaki pants with a white button down shirt, barely buttoned exposing his tanned chest and the sleeves rolled up towards his elbows. His hair in sexy ringlets, curling loosely in various directions: looking wild and wavy.

Realizing he has scared her, he is quick to apologize, "I'm terribly sorry. I didn't intend to frighten you. Please forgive me."

She smiles and opens the screen door, "I've been wondering about you. I thought maybe I managed to make you sick of seeing me," says Taylor.

He kisses her gently on the cheek, his voice soft and sultry; "I could spend every second of my life with you and never would I be sick of you."

He lingers closely, his breath caressing her neck as her heart beats hard within her chest. Her hands grip along his biceps as she pulls him closer to her. Wrapping his arms around her waist, taking in the sweet scent of her skin; the urge to hold onto her forever drives a yearning inside of him that cuts so sharply.

In this special place, within his arms, is the safest place she has ever been; with the existence of no fears. In a small whisper, her voice remarks, "I love you, Alex; always."

He holds onto her even tighter, kissing her softly on the neck, he says, "As I love you too."

As their embrace separates they look steadily into each other's eyes, feeling the other's passion, heartbeats and connection. Taking her hand in his, placing it against the cheek of his face; he feels the contours of her small fingers.

She moves closer, kissing his lips softly. In a swift motion their embrace goes from soft and subtle to untamed passion; crashing against the bookcase, knocking a vase to the floor. The wildness soars within them. Taking a firm grasp on his shirt, she rips it open taking him momentarily by surprise.

He runs his hand up her leg all the way to her thigh, moving underneath her sundress, grasping onto the delicate lacey material of her thong panties destroying them as they break away from her body. Briskly, she pulls her sundress off exposing her small, round firm breasts.

The sheer beauty of her natural form sets him afire, yearning for each and every touch from her hands and mouth. The touch of her sheer skin against his, the brilliant slow moves of her body brushing up against his and her breasts coming ever so closely towards him, becomes far more than he is capable of enduring.

Alex picks her up in his strong arms, holding onto her tightly; he carries her upstairs to the tree house as he pleasures her with every fiber of himself, aware giving nothing less would be acceptable.

Gently he sets her down on top of the bed, hovering over her teasingly with little kisses that begin on her warm lips and slowly run down her neck, over her breasts and down to her belly button. Just as she senses he is returning to her she feels his wet lips kissing her inner thighs causing her adrenaline to intensify.

His mouth pleasures her unlike anything she has ever experienced. She grips the sheets pulling them into a mess around her body, discovering she is unable to control her own body as she climaxes within his hold.

Gasping for air she pulls him back up towards her, holding on tightly. She feels his excitement as his body becomes rigid. Becoming one with each other the rhythm is set in motion, focusing on one another; ignoring the stagnant heat and the sound of the front door as it slowly opens.

Suddenly and without warning, Taylor hears her name being called from another part of the house, "Taylor, where are you?" Downstairs Jonathan stands holding a ripped shirt, his wife's ripped panties and her sundress. A look of pure hostility and anger burn in his eyes as the realization of his wife's infidelity is now a certainty.

Sitting up alarmed and frightened, she frantically pleads with Alex, "It's Jonathan! Please, you have to leave right away, he can't find you here. Please hurry. Go down the balcony steps, quickly!"

Hesitantly he picks up his clothes and rushes down the steps leaving her in a way he didn't intend; alone, vulnerable and to face a man he knew no longer made her happy or felt love for her the same as he.

As Alex races towards the beach, with each step getting him further from the property, Jonathan walks into the tree house to see his wife in the shadows wrapped in a sheet. He walks slowly towards the bed, with his hands held behind his back. He smiles and leans over, kissing Taylor on the cheek, "Hi, baby. Are you surprised to see me?" asks Jonathan.

Scared and intimidated, her voice falters, "Yes. Why didn't you call me from the airport? I would have picked you up."

Running his left hand through her hair, tugging at it tightly, "I didn't want to disturb you and I guess it's a good thing I didn't call because obviously you've been quite busy." He drops Alex's shirt on her lap, "Taylor! Who are you cheating on me with?! Where is he?!"

Standing up, she pleads, "Jonathan, he is nobody. I'm sorry."

Suddenly he begins to laugh in a deep and possessed tone, as if he has been told a very humorous joke, "Taylor, do you honestly think "sorry" is going to cut it? Had your accomplice not had an opportunity to flee, I would have my hands around his neck right now! I'm married to such a conniving bitch. Here I put all my faith in you and in us to have this end up being the thanks I get for it."

Jonathan pauses, thinking and taking in everything. Taylor stands quietly, shaking in fear as she knows she has done the unthinkable and now has no idea of what may lie ahead for her. Without offering her any warning or time to react, he strikes her across the face, knocking her to the floor. Her head hits the bed frame as she hits the floor, knocking her unconscious.

The anger and betrayal boil from within and with no rhyme or reason, he begins kicking his defenseless wife in the stomach and legs repeatedly, using her body as a punching bag in venting his rage and frustration; not taking any notice as to how violent his blows are to her small frame or to acknowledge she is unconscious. By the time he stops himself, she lays bruised and bleeding from her mouth and nose.

Suddenly Jonathan contemplates he may have enough time to catch up with Taylor's male counterpart. Racing down the balcony stairs, leaving his wife maimed and out cold on the tree house floor, he races down the beach in hopes of finding him in order to do far worse to the misfortunate male that has preyed on his wife.

With the beach desolate and no one in sight, as the moon hides behind the clouds leaving shadows on the sand and water; he walks back towards the house. Unbeknownst to Jonathan, Alex nearly back to his house stops and begins putting his clothes back on.

As he gets his shorts and pants on, he picks his shoes up from the sand, horrified at the realization he doesn't have his shirt and the startling recollection of where it remains, inside the house.

Knowing there will be no way Taylor could ever explain its presence and the unlikelihood of it going unnoticed; he turns back and begins running towards the house, hoping he isn't too late to rescue her and bring her back with him; what he had wanted to do all along. No matter what consequences would result from his actions, he will bring her back.

As Alex reaches the villa, he pauses not hearing a sound from the darkened house. He ponders over what he should do, wondering if he should attempt to find a way through a window or leave her alone. His heart anxiously pleads with him to pursue desired actions of finding her, while logic stands firm within to leave things alone, not to make matters worse for her by placing her in jeopardy. In the end, he decides to leave the scene in hopes of preventing Taylor from having a confrontation with her husband.

As he walks the stretch of beach heading home, Alex feels saddened and distraught. His heart aches, for he has never felt this way before, to yearn and long for someone with no choice but to go on without her. He can't help but feel as though he has turned his back on her, abandoning her in her hour of need.

Now, in hindsight he wished he had stayed and stood his ground, to profess his love for her. Jonathan doesn't deserve her; he takes her for granted and no longer treasures her for all the special things that make her who she is.

As the night passes, Taylor is awakened by a sharp throbbing pain on the left side of her head. Her entire body pulsates and aches; feeling like the aftermath of a car accident. The slightest movement causes her to cringe; in sheer pain and agony.

In the darkened room, she lies still and quiet, trembling with fear having no way of knowing if she is in the room alone or not. She knew from memory that the shadows of furniture meant she was in one of the spare bedrooms. Carefully, sliding her hand across the bed to see if Jonathan was beside her; to her relief, she discovers he isn't; so carefully she turns a small lamp on.

As she scans the room before her, she knows she isn't dressed as her naked body rests under the cool sheets. Near the bed, a bathrobe rests on a chair. Just a few feet away, getting to it was another issue. With determination, she struggles to lower her bruised legs off the bed and pull her painful body upwards in a sitting position. Each movement sends stabbing pains throughout her body.

The pain becomes too much, causing her to lower back down on the bed. Pulling the covers back over her body; she begins to cry quietly, sad and fearful of the situation she now faces, she continues crying until she dozes off to sleep.

CHAPTER 12

DAWN OF A NEW DAY

T HE NEXT morning, Jonathan walks quietly into Taylor's room and as he stands at the foot of her bed watching her as she sleeps, he finds it difficult to not look upon his wife with resentment and contempt; even with the knowledge he has betrayed her for years. His infidelity isn't so much an issue in his eyes as for hers, for he always felt he guarded her well enough to prevent such an act from occurring.

As he walks closer, reaching out moving a strand of hair away from her face; she opens her eyes, startled by him hovering over her; feverishly she sits upright, backing up against the headboard. He forces a smile, "You need to get up and start moving around. I'll help you downstairs. We will not discuss what happened, we will move forward. I only hope you've learned a valuable lesson from this entire experience. If there is a next time, I guarantee you won't walk away from it."

Jonathan picks her robe up off the chair and hands it to her, he adds, "Get up and put your robe on. We're going downstairs; you're going to need my help." Trusting him is not something she senses she can do; at this moment in time, she can envision him pushing her down the stairs instead of coming to her aid. None the less, she does as he asks and struggles to an upright standing position.

Surprisingly, Jonathan finds himself feeling shameful in his wife's state and appearance, realizing he inflicted so much damage on her as he looks at her battered body. Without saying a word, he goes to her side and gently aides her in getting downstairs. Placing her on the sofa, he goes to the kitchen and returns with a tray consisting of tea and the breakfast he has prepared for her.

As he sits across from her, his eyes fixated on her. She can only wonder what thoughts line his mind, however, yet too fearful to ask. Returning from where he was lost, he speaks softly yet in a reserved tone, "I have a few errands I must take care of this morning. I have to place my faith in you that you will not disappoint me again. Under no circumstances are you to make any efforts to contact the man you've been sleeping with. If you do, I'll know about it be assured. While I'm gone you need to get back upstairs, bathe and get dressed. Is this understood?"

She replies in a weak trembling voice, "Yes, I understand." Sensing his reluctance to leave she sits quietly, staring down to the floor.

As he prepares to leave, Jonathan stands up walking over to Taylor; crouching in front of her, looking up into her eyes, "I love you no matter what you think of me right now. I would kill or die for you; there isn't anything I wouldn't do for you. I'll be back shortly."

He kisses her gently on the forehead before leaving. As she hears the sound of the car starting up, tears roll down her cheeks uncontrollably. She can't help but feel no matter what happens the short time she spent with Alex was worth it, because for once in her life she was able to experience a love so pure and true that nothing else could ever compare to it.

She struggles to her feet; making her way back upstairs. With every step a sharp pain is sent pulsating from her stomach and legs. Doing her best to think outside of her pain she knows she must obey his direction and make progress before he returns.

Jonathan arrives in town, making a stop by the local police department. Sergeant Glenn Turpin; an elderly man, more like a fixture of the department than an actual active member, greets him when he walks inside; "Look who's here! Jonathan Reed, it has been awhile. How long have you been in town?"

Jonathan smiles and shakes the sergeant's hand, replying "I got in last night, how are things going at this end of the world?"

Sergeant Turpin tilts his head, "Oh, not much mostly petty crime. This area remains less populated than the outlying cities, which I'm thankful for. Did you bring that pretty little wife with you?"

Jonathan struggles to maintain a positive composure, "Taylor is here. Actually, she has been here for awhile now. She came without me. I couldn't break away from work as I had originally intended to."

The sergeant smiles, "Being a powerful and big time lawyer has its disadvantages I guess. She should have stopped by. Had I known the little lady was here alone, I would have offered surveillance around the property to make sure she felt safe. I'm sure she's glad you're here."

Rubbing his temple, Jonathan replies, "Well, Glenn that I'm not too sure about. Apparently, while I've been in New York, she has met someone here. I don't know for how long they have been in each other's company and I don't know anything about the fellow. I was hoping maybe she has been spotted around town with him and you or someone else would know his identity."

Sergeant Turpin appears puzzled by the news, "I'm sorry, Jonathan, I have no idea who it would be. I didn't even know she was in town. If she has been going out then it's likely she has been visiting other areas. I can look into it for you, if you'd like."

Appearing disappointed, Jonathan continues, "No, there's no bother. I'm sure I'll cross paths with him sooner or later. I'll see you around, Glenn."

Just as Jonathan is about to leave, the sergeant speaks up, "Will you and Taylor be attending the Tunstall Ball tomorrow evening? It is always the biggest event of the year; always a big hit."

Jonathan turns back, forcing a smile, he says "Thanks for reminding me, I wouldn't want to miss it. I have a lot of people to reconnect with while we're here. I look forward to seeing you there. I better get back to Taylor, she isn't feeling well. Don't want to leave her for too long."

The sergeant's voice carries as he walks away, "Give the little Mrs. my best."

Jonathan drives back to the villa, displeased that he is still no closer at discovering the identity of the man who managed to bed his wife.

Inside, Taylor has managed to take a hot shower and dress herself. Making it back downstairs to the kitchen, she begins making lunch at the counter. With the sudden sound of the door opening, she clumsily drops the large kitchen knife she was about to cut the sandwiches in half with.

Struggling to crouch down to pick it back up, Jonathan bends down picking it up from the floor before she can get anywhere near reaching it. Seeing the knife in his hand as the point sticks outward, the unknown intent of her husband sends chills down her spine.

He lays the knife down in the sink while gently placing his other hand against the small of her back. Her body trembles to his touch as he stands close behind her, with his mouth close to her left ear. She can feel each exhale warming the side of her neck as he moves closer and begins kissing her neck, he asks, "Did you miss me?"

It takes everything she has to calm herself from the anxiety she is experiencing, to reply, "Yes, dear. I did miss you." His Jekyll and Hyde personality traits had taken their toll on her. His sudden change in demeanor and temperament kept her guessing as to which she would see next. Now she found herself taking the outlook that if in fact he wished to kill her, she preferred that he do it and let it be done and over. The abuse and imprisonment was too much for her to bear any longer.

Jonathan pulls a beautiful bouquet of red roses around in front of Taylor, "These are for you. I know they won't make up for what I've done and the horrible way I've behaved, yet they are a start, a start to a new us, a better and improved us. I've done a great deal of soul searching. I haven't been there for you in the past few years and I've managed to forsake you to put more emphasis on my career. Winning this case has done a great deal to further me in the firm. I'm going to spend more time at home and I think we should begin making plans to have a family."

Taylor turns around, looking at Jonathan. He smiles at her, as he continues, "I know you'd make an excellent mother and I'm ready to be a father. I truly think it would be a glorious thing to embark upon. We can get a house on the outskirts of town. It's time to stop procrastinating on plans we set out to partake in years ago."

She smiles back, "Are you sure you're ready for such big steps?"

He laughs, "Of course, I've been selfish in making you wait this long. I love you, Taylor. It's time that I make dreams come true with you. You've stood by while I made mine a reality. I want this more than you could ever know."

Jonathan's eyes turn from warm to cold in seconds, he says, "I will say this to you only once. Whomever you were seeing while I was away, you are not to contact him in any way, shape or form and if he attempts to contact you, for your sake you best not utter a word or glance to him. Any indiscretion on your part and that will seal your fate. I will not be made a fool of again, not by you or anyone else. Is that clear?"

Tired of the inquisition, she replies wearily, "Yes, Jonathan, I understand and I will not do anything to hurt you. I've let you down; betraying your trust. I can't expect you to ever forgive me."

Hugging her, he holds her tightly, "You're human. You made a mistake and yes, you hurt me, but I meant the vows I made to you when we married. We will get through this together and we'll become stronger because of it."

The following day, Taylor begins to feel better. Her pains and aches begin to subside. As she stands before the large mirror in the master bedroom, she studies her bruised face; a black eye, cut on her lip and scrapes along her nose. A thing of beauty, she is no longer, for now she looks as though she had been in a powerful boxing match of which she was not the victor. She realized it would be awhile before she'd be able to venture out, surely only by the accompaniment of Jonathan.

As the afternoon sun shines in through the open windows, a gentle breeze floats throughout the house. Preparing lunch, Taylor thinks about Alex; wondering how he is and if he misses her as much as she misses him. Brushing him from mind was easier said than done. How do you forget the person who has altered your world and perception of what love truly means?

Wrapping his arms around her, Jonathan rests his chin on her shoulder, "I'm going to take a quick swim. I won't be long. I'll be back in time for lunch."

Before leaving he adds, "Oh, I don't know how long I'll be at the ball tonight. I'll try to cut the evening short. I don't think you should be alone, so I've asked Sara Jackson to come over while I'm out."

Taylor looks at her husband; hoping to give a compassionate argument against having an adult sitter, she argues, "Jonathan that really isn't necessary. I'm not going anywhere and I assure you I'm not going to do anything foolish."

Jonathan quickly interjects, "I have the entire thing covered. I've told her you took a tumble down the steps carrying too much in your arms and you're bruised from the fall. She will be here at 6:00. I wouldn't go, but you know this is a very important business opportunity."

Feeling anxious and uneasy about being placed in a situation of display, Taylor uneasily does the best she can to cover her bruises; wearing jeans and an oversized shirt. Jonathan, dressed to kill in his black tuxedo, walks downstairs just as the doorbell rings. Opening the door, Sara, a blonde who is thirty-seven years old with her leathery tanned skin and local accent stands smiling, "Jonathan, hello it's so good to see you again. You look very handsome tonight in your duds. Where's Taylor?"

He smiles, motioning for her to come inside, "She's upstairs, she'll be down in a few minutes. She is still pretty sore from the fall."

Taylor comes downstairs, smiling at Sara; hugging her distant friend, "Hi, it's so good to see you," says Taylor.

Sara replies, "Had I known you had been here for awhile, I would have called and taken you to lunch or shopping."

Taylor glances over Sara's shoulder at Jonathan, who looks at her with an expression of hindsight and knowledge of the truth. Taylor continues, "I'm so happy you're here."

Sara looks sympathetically at Taylor, "You poor dear, you are banged up pretty roughly. How did it happen? I mean, I know you fell down the stairs."

Glancing briefly at her husband, she begins to detail the lie to cover up the truth, "I thought I could carry an oversized basket of towels downstairs to the wash and ended up slipping on the second stair from the top. The worst was the first two days, I'm feeling better today," says Taylor.

Looking at his watch, Jonathan kisses Taylor on the cheek, "Alright girls, I've got to go. Thanks Sara for keeping Taylor company while I'm out. I'll be back as soon as I can."

As the two girls begin to plan out their evening, they sit with a glass of wine on the sofa. Sara offers, "Can I get you anything? What would you like to do?"

Taylor smiles, "No thank you, Sara, I'm fine. I actually took a pain pill a bit ago and odds are it will knock me out for the rest of the evening. I've had difficulty sleeping and this is the only thing that helps. I truly feel terrible that Jonathan asked you to sit with me. I'm sure you have more interesting things to do during the evening, than sit and watch me sleep."

Sara aims to smile, but the realization that what Taylor says is in fact true and doesn't escape from her facial expression, "Oh, I don't mind. I'll be here in case you wake up and need anything."

Taylor assures Sara, "Oh, I won't be waking up that is not until morning, once I've had these pills, I don't wake back up at all. Sara, if you find yourself bored; feel free to leave at any time. Jonathan will be back in a few hours so I won't be here alone for long."

Taylor desperately longs for her babysitter to leave, knowing this is her only chance to contact Alex. The window of opportunity will not stay open for long, it has to be now.

At the ball, Jonathan mingles in the large crowd of people at the exquisite ballroom, rich and alive with history from timeless paintings, furniture to priceless artifacts. A room full of history and a glorious past. Rich socialites walk up to Jonathan; Claire and Fred Childress from Las Vegas, Nevada, "Jonathan, I'm so pleased to see you made it this year. How are you?" Claire inquires.

He takes her satin gloved hand in his, kissing it in greeting, "I'm very well, thank you. Claire, you look stunning this evening, as always." The older female who has taken every available measure to remain looking youthful, from plastic surgery to injections: smiles warmly at the compliment.

Jonathan's eyes move to her husband, Fred, as he offers him a firm handshake, "Fred, it's great to see you. How's business going in Vegas? I keep telling Taylor, we really must get down there soon."

Fred's face lights up, "Oh, you must. I can introduce you to a great deal of clientele and give you a chance to play a golf course you've never had the pleasure of playing. The wives can go shopping. That is what Claire prides herself on."

The couple laughs, as Fred suddenly spots someone nearing in the crowd, he motions to the man in the distance to come over, "Oh, I almost forgot, there's someone here I'd like to introduce you to. This guy is great, very wealthy, he's international. Maybe you can add him to your client base."

Alex steps into the circle, smiling at Claire and looking at Fred, he says, "Hi, Fred."

Fred makes the introduction, "Jonathan Reed, this is Alex Parker. Alex owns and operates his family's restructuring company in London. Alex, Jonathan here is a high powered attorney in New York."

Jonathan holds out his hand to Alex who has fallen into the realization that Taylor's husband is standing before him, quickly he offers his hand and forces a smile, replying "It's a pleasure to make your acquaintance."

Jonathan smiles, "I don't believe I've seen you here before. Are you new to the island?"

Alex replies, "No, actually this is the first time I've been graciously invited. My family and I own a home on the beach."

Jonathan smiles as Claire speaks up, "Jonathan, I just realized, Taylor isn't with you. Where is she?"

He turns his focus back to her, "Oh, Claire, she truly wanted to attend; however, she had an accident a few days ago. She's at home resting."

A look of concern forms on Claire's face, as she comments, "Oh, dear, I do hope she is alright."

Jonathan smiles, "Oh, she'll be fine. She fell down the stairs carrying too much in her arms at one time." Jonathan looks at Alex, continuing, "My wife, Taylor, she is often clumsy, not watching where she's going."

Claire chimes in again, "I will give her a call, and we'll go to lunch."

Alex's heart races, he knows he must see her immediately. Standing so close to her evil husband he begins to feel his adrenaline increase and his anger boiling from within, making him feel sick to his stomach.

Offering his hand to Jonathan, Alex remarks, "Jonathan, it was a pleasure to meet you. I must speak to someone I just saw go past."

As Alex walks away into the crowd, Jonathan appears disappointed and offended by his lack of interest. Jonathan calls out to Alex, "Find me later; I'd really like to discuss some representation elements for you and your company."

Alex smiles back, "Sure thing."

Fred remarks, "Alex is a great guy, has homes all over the world: Quite wealthy."

Back at the villa, Taylor sleeps on the sofa while the movie plays. Sara walks over and bends down to check on Taylor, asking softly "Taylor, do you need anything?" She doesn't respond, again she calls out, "Taylor". She doesn't move or wake. Sara decides she has had enough of watching Taylor sleep, coming to the conclusion she can't be of much help since she was now induced into a medicated sleep.

Before leaving she writes on a piece of paper to Jonathan explaining that Taylor feel asleep after taking pain medication and she stayed for awhile before leaving her. For him to call if there's anything she can do and then turning off the television, she quietly leaves.

A short time later, Taylor is aroused to hear an unrelenting knock at the door. Steadily she rises and makes her way to the door. Her heart plummets as she sees Alex standing before her, "Alex! Hi, what are you doing here?"

He gazes at her, his heart sinking at the sight of the cuts and bruises on her, "After meeting your husband just a short time ago, I knew I had to come see you."

Bewildered she asks, "You met Jonathan?"

He smiles, "Yes, I'm afraid so, at the ball. I was hoping you had accompanied him and then I learned from his lips alone that you had an accident and fell." She glances away, unable to look truthfully in his eyes from the lie to cover up the truth.

Alex asks firmly, "You didn't fall, did you? He did this to you, didn't he?"

Touching his hand, she contends, "Alex, it isn't important, what is important is that we have this time no matter how brief to see each other once more and I'm so thankful for this."

He moves closer, touching her gently on the face, his brown eyes piercing a hole in her heart, "Taylor, your husband is of no importance to me; however, you are. When we parted I made a huge mistake in leaving without you. I'm not going to make that mistake again."

Sensing the sincerity from the expression on his face, she argues, "I can't leave with you. If I were to, we would never be safe and we'd always be looking over our shoulder until one day he would be standing before us, because he would not stop until he found us and killed us both."

Alex pleads with her intensely to prove to her otherwise, "I would never allow that to happen. I can keep us a step ahead. I'd go to the ends of the earth for you and protect you always. I promise. If you stay with him your days will remain marked. If he is able to take no distress in beating you, then to kill you would only take a little more effort. I will not leave you behind to die at his hands. If you choose to stay then I must stay as well and await his return, to profess my love for you. I will not be without you."

Taylor begins crying, knowing what wrath awaits them if Jonathan discovers them together and knowing Alex's sincerity and passion, she knows he isn't bluffing; she pleads, "Alex, please. I can't allow you to place yourself in harms way for me."

Alex quickly interjects, "Then come with me now. We'll leave tonight, go right to the airport. We can be gone before he gets home."

She debates in her mind whether to leave or stay before making her decision, "We have to hurry. He'll make efforts to get back as quickly as he can and he may call to see if Sara is still here."

Taylor looks for her purse as Alex looks helpless, "What can I do?" he asks.

Realizing it won't take much to make a quick getaway; she replies to him, "I have a suitcase in the upstairs hallway closet that I haven't unpacked. Grab it for me and we can go." He races up the stairs as if racing against someone else; frantically searching the closet, grabbing the suitcase, running back downstairs to Taylor.

Helping her to the car, he quickly races off in the direction of his beach house. With worry and concern in her tone, she asks "Alex is this going to work?"

He grabs hold of her left hand, "Don't worry. You will never spend another moment with him again or be in fear, ever again. I vow this to you, I will make you so happy more than you can ever imagine possible."

Knowing time is of the essence; Alex makes a call to his pilot, Nigel Rutger, "Nigel, I will be leaving this evening for Charleston. I need you to have the plane fueled and ready to go in an hour. I must leave immediately. Thank you."

Staring out the window into the darkness she begins to fear she has made a dreadful mistake and doubts they'll safely be able to leave before being discovered. Knowing Jonathan, he will have the entire town looking for them in minutes. Alex tugs at her hand getting her attention, "We'll be gone before you know it. I don't want you to regret the choice you've made by leaving with me."

While Alex frantically gathers his things that he cannot leave without, Taylor sits in the living room waiting patiently and quietly staring at the clock on the wall, knowing time will soon run out for the both of them. Each second brings Jonathan that much closer to finding them. Fearing she has made the largest mistake of her life, she contemplates racing down the beach in hopes of making it back before Jonathan.

Knowing Alex's love for her, he would throw caution to the wind that much she knew but felt uncertain this was something she could be okay with, if it led him into danger. He was willing to sacrifice everything, even life for her; how could she ever repay him for such boundless love and devotion? Her heart plummets inside her chest, falling as far as it can. She races to the patio doors, holding tightly to the handle seriously contemplating fleeing before its too late.

Alex rushes into the room with his belongings, noticing Taylor holding tightly to the sliding glass door. He walks over to her immediately, wrapping an arm around her waist as if to hold her back from what she is considering, "Please don't leave. I know I can't stop you if it is what you truly want, but I don't believe it is. I would never have come to you tonight if I didn't feel otherwise. I know not everything in life has certainties but this does, we do. I don't want to move forward without you."

She lets go of the door and turns to him, with tears in her eyes, "I do love you that I can't deny. Walking out of my marriage is something I never envisioned myself doing and living in fear is all I know, so I have doubts on how this will play out. Pulling you into this is an uncertainty for me."

Holding her close, he says softly, "Don't think about it in that way. We're going to leave here tonight and no one will find you, not him, not anyone. We'll make a life together; a fresh start."

···━◆▶···

As they arrive at the airport, Alex drives along the tarmac up to the area of a leer jet plane, with a well-dressed pilot standing tall by the stairs. Her eyes widen at the sight of the luxurious craft unable to fathom it belonging to Alex, "Is this yours?"

He smiles widely, "Yes, we will be flying in style my dear. I wouldn't have it any other way. The bags will have to be checked and loaded before we can take off. It won't take long. You can wait for me aboard the plane. Nigel will take care of you."

As they approach the plane, Taylor begins to feel a sense of relief and more at ease. The pilot smiles at the couple; greeting them, "Good evening, sir. Hello, madam."

Alex introduces Taylor, "Nigel, this is Taylor. She will be accompanying me. Please see that she has anything she needs."

Directing his hands towards the plane, "Shall we? I'll show you the inside of the plane if you'd like."

She smiles, "Thank you."

Alex removes his bags and briefcase from the car as Taylor gets a tour of the plane. Once on board, Alex finds her looking out the window and smiling joyfully as he approaches her. His heart cries out each time he looks at her scarred beauty, wondering how any man could strike such a beautiful and loving woman. If he could have his way, he would take Jonathan down himself; leaving him to recover from his inflicted blows.

He points to the seat beside Taylor, "Is this seat taken?"

She smiles, "Why I'm afraid it is. I am saving it for the man I love; the keeper of my heart."

His eyes glisten, "To hold your heart is a profound gift. He is a very lucky man." Fixated on his eyes she concurs, "Yes, you are but not as nearly as lucky as I." He sits down beside her, holding her hand gently in his.

Seeing his car outside the window, "What happens to your car?" I have a caretaker who will take it back to the property. I have groundskeepers for each home. I'm not at most of them for long periods of time, so they have to be maintained by someone else. My flat in London is the most used of them all."

Alex continues, "Over time, you'll see all of them. We are going to Charleston first, for awhile anyway. I recently purchased a plantation property there. It is quite beautiful, completely renovated to capture the essence of its original style and beauty, yet partially updated. I must confess; this will be my first time seeing it since acquiring the property. I had the decorator make the changes I wanted while I was in London."

She lays her head on his shoulder, "I've never been to Charleston before. I haven't had an opportunity to do much traveling. I'm sure I'll love it. I would love anywhere with you."

He kisses her forehead, "It will be perfect. We'll make a home for ourselves there."

After having several failed attempts at getting an answer at the villa, Jonathan politely excuses himself from his current company and races home. Anger and hostility run throughout him, sensing Taylor is up to no good. Stopping the car in front of the house he places it in park and exits the car without turning it off or shutting the door, stepping angrily towards the door.

As he opens the door, he stands at the entrance calling Taylor's name loudly as he surveys the stairs, the kitchen, and the living room, knowing deep down she isn't going to emerge from any of the locations. The house is eerily quiet and solemn. Foolishly he thought he could put faith and trust in her once again only to be made the fool.

Spotting the piece of paper left on a table near the door, he picks it up and reads it. Angrily he erupts from within as he grabs the phone, calling Sara. She answers, "Hello."

Franticly he says, "Sara, this is Jonathan. How long ago did you leave Taylor?"

She hears the anxiousness in his tone, she replies, "I left her sleeping about two hours ago. She was resting. She had taken pain medication and said she wouldn't wake back up. Is everything alright? Do you need for me to come back over?"

Unable to control his anger, he explodes over the phone "No, she isn't here. If by chance she contacts you, please call me immediately. I'll have my cell phone with me. I'm going to look for her."

Sensing by his tone, his hostility, she says; "Jonathan, I'm so sorry. I feel terrible for leaving."

Jonathan hangs up. Thoughts race through his head, wondering where she went and how long she has been gone.

He knows the odds are she is in the arms of her lover, whom he has managed to learn nothing about. Time would now be crucial. He has to find her before its too late. He calls Detective Rally Walton, a close friend on the island. "Rally, this is Jonathan Reed. I'm in the area. I have a huge problem and favor to ask you."

The detective replies quickly, "Just name it."

Jonathan continues, "Taylor is missing. She met someone; I don't know his name or who he is. She has run off with him and I have to track her down. I need for you to find her. I don't know how long they'll stay in the area."

Sensing the alarm in his voice, Rally replies, "Don't you worry, I'll find her."

"Thanks, Rally; I have my cell with me. Keep me posted."

"You bet," says the detective before ending the call.

Impatiently Jonathan races down the beach, hoping to find her there. Knowing Taylor, his better judgment tells him she is gone this time and won't return on her own. The thoughts of her off with another man cut him to his core. This is the last straw, he has given her so much and so many second chances only to have her offer such deceit in return.

Mistakenly, he thought she understood him and had enough sense to mind him, no matter if she left of her own free will or was talked into leaving, he now knew he had to take care of her once and for all. To make a huge fool of him was not going to happen, under no circumstances.

CHAPTER 13

A NEW DAY, A FRESH START

I N CHARLESTON, South Carolina, the plane lands and the two enter a limousine that waits for them at the gate. Taylor finds herself unable to remove herself from the view outside her window, anxiously taking in all the sights as they drive past.

Silently Alex looks on, pleased at her wonderment and child-like enthusiasm at her new surroundings. As he held her throughout the night aboard the plane, he knew he made the right decision. There was a great deal left to take care of and being the brilliant businessman he was, he knew it would have to be handled quickly and with the utmost discretion.

If the two of them were to begin a life together, she would have to have no ties to her past. He wasn't sure if she fathomed the extremity of the choice she made, but he had. She would not be able to contact anyone in her past and she would have to be cautious on all accounts, for any slight error in judgment would lead Jonathan right to them.

All he could think was how he needed to reach his friend, Graham Rosser and press him on creating a new identity for her. It would be their only hope in her being able to become a new person, with no ties to the past. If he couldn't help them, Alex knew he'd find someone who could, whether it is someone in illegal dealings or not. One way or another he would make it happen, he was rich and money wouldn't be an issue.

As the car rounds the edge of the massive estate, turning down the long tree-lined lane leading to the house, Taylor is in awe at its beauty and the wonderment of the past it holds captive in every limb, each breeze from the enormous weeping willows, and everything else that holds as timeless as history bestows.

The lane itself is long and surrounded by tall oak and weeping willow trees, hiding the house from the main stretch of road. As they near the house, the majestic view is so brilliant and amazing that Taylor doesn't wait for the driver to come around to open her door; she steps out and moves towards the property as if drawn to it.

The large home is a two level with doors leading out to a balcony from up above. The house had to belong to a large southern family she imagined for it had so many rooms, which she could easily identify from the outside. The yard was well kept and the garden of various arrays of shrubs and plants added to its beauty and design.

Rushing to Alex's side, she impatiently asks, "Alex, may we go inside?"

He smiles at her, "Of course, you go on ahead and I'll be right behind you," says Alex enthusiastically. She smiles as she walks up the stairs leading to the entrance of the house, slowly opening the door as if not wanting to disturb or rush into it.

As the two enter the magnificent house, rich with history and memories, she discovers it amazes her with every fine detail and charming quality; beginning with the large entranceway resting underneath a second story balcony supported by four very large and sturdy beams.

The old fashioned sitting room at the entrance still reflects a time lost and long forgotten. The antique furniture lines the walls in perfect unison; whereas no other accommodations could compliment it as well. A spiral staircase near the front door, leads upstairs to numerous rooms.

Before exploring upstairs, she walks delicately to each of the rooms downstairs, intrigued to make a visit to each one to make her introduction. Alex follows a few steps behind, quietly enjoying her delight and overwhelming thrills at their new surroundings.

From the card room, small and large scale dining rooms, to the kitchen which has recently been remodeled with a more updated version of appliances and cabinetry.

Out into the magnificent back yard with a stone walkway and patio, seated with various outdoor arrangements and a lush garden of splendid plants and shrubs: complimenting the house even more so than the display in front.

Entering the rooms upstairs she feels a bit awkward, as though entering into someone else's room; a sense that the previous occupants left it just as they wished upon their return. Canopy beds fill each room with small two seated sitting tables, a sofa placed near each fireplace and nightstands at each bedside.

She glances at Alex, with a smile; he says with a grin, "It is your pick of which room. I leave that choice up to you."

Looking around the current room being visited, she remarks, "I feel as though it isn't a choice for us to make as though each room is still occupied by a previous tenant."

Resting his arms around her waist and resting his head gently upon her left shoulder, he surveys the room, Alex says, "My dear, I feel it too. I guess I may have kept a bit too much of the original furnishings. It isn't quite resonating new ownership. How about we make due with it tonight and tomorrow we'll go into town and do some shopping of our own?"

Taylor turns to Alex, fearful of giving the wrong idea, "Oh, by no means do I want to imply that the furniture should go for something new. I'm certain by adding a few different touches it would take on an entirely different appeal," remarks Taylor.

He smiles, "I'm certain it will, yet I too am not that comfortable with sleeping in a bed that isn't of my own. So at least for our room, we'll make the room into our own liking and take the other rooms as we go for changes or alterations. Yes?"

As Alex addresses the newly acquired staff, Taylor wanders outside exploring the gardens and the arched wooden bridge crossing over a pond. Standing on the bridge, gazing out over the water, watching as her reflection ripples in the windblown water; her mind begins to wander and a fear grips her so violently, as the sense of danger feels ever so near.

Her mind races with thoughts and images of Jonathan, knowing he has already begun a search for her and knowing no matter how well they think they've covered their tracks, he will in time find them one way or another. He will exhaust every resource he has in order of finding them.

She questions how could she have willingly placed Alex in such danger and although he didn't refuse the complexity or the circumstances that surrounded her, he did not deserve to be brought into such a dangerous scenario. If anything were to happen to Alex, she knew she would never forgive herself.

Her heart wants to be with Alex and it beats for no one else, yet that in itself doesn't accommodate making life threatening decisions in order of obtaining that which her heart so greatly desires. Sensing as though it may not be too late to turn back, still a chance of getting out before it is a lost opportunity; she concludes; she must leave.

Knowing to acknowledge this decision would only allow Alex to talk her out of it and plead with her to stay; she knows with all certainty she must leave him behind and without being able to stop her. Tonight it must be done; she will listen to reason and ignore the pleading of her heart.

Quietly Alex walks up behind Taylor, wrapping his arms across her shoulders clutching loosely as he holds her close; positioning his mouth close to her left ear. She smiles as her eyes remain focused on the water watching as if transfixed on the glittering effects of the light shimmering on the water.

Knowing her fears and mindset, Alex does his best to ease her worries; softly he whispers into her ear, "You're safe here. He won't find you. Trust me, I won't allow anything to happen to you." As he holds her close, she turns in his arms, wrapping her arms around his waist, burying her head in his chest to find solace and reassurance in his embrace.

CHAPTER 14

A TIME FOR CHANGE

THE MONTHS begin to pass, winter leading into spring, it causes a beautiful transformation in the property. The weeping willows and massive old oak trees, with cuffs of Spanish moss line the lane standing firm as if guards lined up in a stance of protection. Flowers bloom throughout the property providing a sweet scent of honeysuckle and lilacs.

Over the winter months, Alex stayed by her side, leaving her only on brief occasions to deal with business that could not be handled any other way; secretly, he feared for her safety. Knowing if he was in Jonathan's position, he too would not sit idly by as someone took Taylor and disappeared.

Alex took every precaution to insure her safety. He had a high tech security system installed in the house and purchased a hand gun and took target practice, just in case a time called for him to use force to protect her.

Alex continually pushes his friend, Graham Rosser, who has connections in obtaining a new identity for Taylor. To his surprise and amazement he comes through providing a new name, social security number and background. Alex has the cook prepare a special dinner for the two of them and asks Taylor to wear a beautiful sheer and flowing open back black dress which ties around her neck.

Sitting together at the smaller dining table, due to Taylor's inability to sustain the distance left between them at the formal dining table, she looks at Alex; who appears to be beaming with a positive vibe, "I can tell you have good news. Would you like to share it with me or allow it to just explode from within?," asks Taylor.

He smiles as he looks at her warmly, knowing he can't wait any longer to tell her the news, Alex responds, "Graham has come through. I owe him dearly for he has created a new identity for you; a new name, background, social security number; a new person for you to become for a new life."

Taylor falls back in her chair as she appears to have difficulty breathing. Alex rushes to her side asking, "Are you alright? What's the matter?"

Struggling to regain composure, she replies, "I just never expected things to go so well. I guess I just assumed some sort of downfall would take place and everything that is so perfect would be lost."

Alex bends down, holding her hand, looking up into her eyes, he says, "I assure you that will not happen. I will take every measure every precaution to keep you safe and happy. I would not have uprooted you and turned your life upside down, had I not the full capacity or determination to keep my word to you." He kisses her on the cheek and returns to his seat.

Holding up his wine glass, he continues, "Lets make a toast; to new beginnings, a new identity, a fresh start, and to your job interview on Monday just two days away."

Taylor looks at him confused, "Job interview?" She asks Alex.

Alex continues, "Oh, did I forget to mention you have an interview scheduled with the principal of the local elementary school? How silly of me. Yes, as you know I've made some contacts here in town and I learned from Carter Preston, the principal of Forest Oak Elementary that they are in need of a kindergarten teacher. I put in a good word for you and he asked that you come in and meet with him. Now, don't get the idea that I've sealed the deal in any manner. I got the interview and now it is up to you to do the rest."

Elated, Taylor rushes over to him forgetting all about the toast, sitting across his lap wrapping her arms around him, kissing him repeatedly, she states joyously, "Thank you, thank you! This means so much to me. I'm truly going to cry. I have wanted this for so long, a job and a career of my own. I have so much to do, plans to make. I have to make a great impression."

He laughs, "I know you will; however, let us have dinner and spend the rest of the evening in celebrating your good news and then tomorrow you can begin preparations for your interview," says Alex.

As the early evening passes, Taylor waits for Alex upstairs in the master bedroom. Standing at the open balcony doors, feeling the warm night air flowing in from the trees lining the lane; she gazes at the moonlit property. With a cocktail in hand, she washes it down quickly in hopes of removing her tempestuous fears of something negative waiting to spoil her good fortune.

Years of having the negative take hold, while with Jonathan, she finds it isn't so easy to change perspective or drop her guard. Alex quietly walks a few feet into the room, standing quietly behind Taylor. With his tie unfastened and the remains of his drink lingering in his glass, he quietly sets his glass down on a table near the doorway.

Approaching her from behind, he slowly moves his right hand across the sheer clothing covering her stomach. His soft, warm lips kiss along her shoulder, as he moves her hair away from her neck, kissing up towards her ear. Lost in his touch, she begins to feel weak in the knees. Turning around, she looks deeply into his eyes sensing the depths of his desire.

He kisses her passionately, pulling her close touching the velvet bare skin of her back. Feeling as if she suddenly becomes possessed by the forces of something unknown, she wildly rips his shirt open. Stunned and taken back, Alex appears caught off guard. She offers him no time to rationalize what is about to take place by unfastening his pants, backing him up towards the bed until he falls backwards onto the bed.

Hovering over top of him, she runs her tongue along his chest down towards his belly button. In a quick change of turn he flips her over onto the bed, holding her arms down with his body pressed firmly against hers. His excitement builds as he presses against her open legs.

Reaching behind her neck, he unfastens the dress exposing her breasts in the bright moonlight. Her eagerness heightens as he begins suckling on her breasts. A strong, warm breeze blows into the room striking them, running wildly through their hair.

From the friction and joined heat of their bodies, droplets of sweat pierce their bodies, rolling down his back, dripping off the ends of his wavy wet ringlets of hair. Coming into her, she trembles briefly as the intensity of anticipation and wanting him begins to give away to the pleasure of becoming one.

Taylor's long, sleek legs wrap around Alex's body as he moves towards her, kissing her briefly in stride as the motions become more rapid and powerful. Constricting his body closer to hers, placing his head next to hers, hovering over her; she holds tightly onto his pulsating arms, feeling his muscles stiffen.

As she reaches her plateau first, Alex feels it then too as her nails pierce the skin of his back. Eager to please and be pleased he shifts his focus, excitement and drive; making a quick second place. His body goes limp as he exhaustedly rests on top of Taylor.

They breathe in the night air feverishly trying to restore the oxygen lost. That night, they lay naked in each others arms: nothing standing in the way of their love for one another or their unison beating hearts. For the first time, Taylor is able to relax and let her worries leave her. She drifts off to sleep with ideals of a new life and future.

On Monday morning, Alex paces back and fourth in the downstairs study; unable to focus on work or think of little else except for Taylor and her job interview. Worrying about her, wondering how she's doing. He desperately wanted to go along for moral support; however, she said she would do far better going alone.

They spent the weekend going over pertinent details; her new name, Beth Jones and educational background; attending NYC obtaining a teaching degree. Alex gave all the support he could before she left, praising her capabilities and his belief in her. After being together day in and day out for so long, his heart dropped from his chest as he stood at the doorway watching helplessly as she drove down the lane away from the house.

Normalcy not yet taking place within their lives they each took daily steps to bring that which they desired, a regular day with average goings on in exchange for the many days of fears and steps walking on a wire. Finally, that moment had arrived. A solid step into acquiring the confidence and security desperately needed to lead a worry-free existence.

Alex hears the front door open; quickly he races to the door to greet Taylor. She needs not to utter a word, he can tell by the disappointed expression on her face things did not go well in the interview. As her eyes meet his, a smile crosses her face and she blurts out, "I got it! I got the job!"

He lifts her up off the floor, holding her in his arms spinning in circles. As he puts her down, he cradles her face in his hands, "I knew you could do it. I'm so happy for you," says Alex.

Taylor quickly begins telling Alex all about it, saying "I was so nervous. I can't explain it but this calm came over me as the interview began and I just knew what I had to do. I stayed focused and on top of every question. I remained friendly and upbeat. It just worked. He offered me the job right then and there. I start right away to get prepared for school to begin in the fall. I now have purpose and it is all because of you. Your encouragement has brought me this far and I owe a world of gratitude to you."

Alex kisses Taylor, "I love you. I look forward to sharing a future together and building on what we have. This is just the start of great things to come," states Alex.

As they make plans to celebrate, back in New York, Jonathan becomes aggravated at the standstill of locating Taylor. In the apartment, Jonathan frantically makes phone calls to the private detective he hired in New York and back to Australia, to speak with Sergeant Glenn Turpin. "Glenn, this is Jonathan Reed; have you had any leads turn up on Taylor?"

"No, Mr. Reed. It is as though she vanished off the face of the earth. We have had no reports of anyone in the area seeing her leave. I've checked the boating areas of the night she disappeared and the airport. There were no flights connecting to New York on that evening," remarks the sergeant.

Jonathan presses further, "Odds are she wouldn't return to New York. She would have traveled with this person somewhere further away than New York. Were there any other flights out with sets of couples?"

Glenn Turpin continues, "Around the time she went missing there were four flights leaving the airport, one heading towards Africa, one to Japan, one to Florida and a private plane headed towards to United States; its destination is unknown."

Suspicious, Jonathan inquires about the plane, "Who is the owner of the private plane?"

"That would be Alex Parker III. He is a wealthy businessman from London, who owns property here," says Glenn. The name rings a bell; he knows he has heard the name before. His mind races to recall where or under what circumstances.

Jonathan pleads for more information on Alex, "Glenn, do you know anything more on this Alex guy?"

A brief pause goes over the line, as the sergeant recalls, "I've met him a few times, he's a young fellow. He has dark wavy hair, brown eyes, British. He mentioned to me once that he mainly stays in London where his family's business is located; yet he did say he owns several other properties in the United States. He didn't mention a wife or kids."

Jonathan replies, "Thanks, Glenn. This is helpful information. I appreciate all you've done. I'll be in touch."

Before he hangs up, the sergeant adds, "I just realized something. Mr. Parker's place is only a few miles down the beach from your place. It would be within walking distance. Are you thinking Taylor met him and he's the one she ran off with?"

The utmost anger and rage begins to pump within Jonathan's veins as he hears his inner suspicions confirmed by someone else. He quickly ends the call, "I'll be in touch." As he sits at his desk, looking over at the photo of him and Taylor, his eyes fixate on her as the hostility grows deeper and deeper.

Picking the phone receiver back up, not taking his gaze off the photo. He dials a phone number. Jonathan begins, "I have important information in our search. I know who she's with. His name is Alex Parker III. He left in a private jet from Australia on the night she disappeared. Find out where that plane landed and find where he has her. I wanted this information yesterday."

He hangs up the phone. Picking up the photo, his jaw line becomes tighter as he gazes at his photo of her awhile longer. In one quick motion he throws it against the wall, shattering the glass from the frame. Over the past months, his life has spiraled out of control.

Falling from grace, he managed to lose his promising promotion, forced to take a leave of absence from all he has ever known, the successful career which had always defined him. His affair was finally put to rest; as now all he could consume himself with was locating Taylor.

He could not rest until he had her back in his life. The resentment he was unable to escape dwelled in the fact of her abandonment. After all of their years together, he could not make sense of how she could just throw it all away to run off with someone in order to get away from him.

Jonathan knew he wasn't perfect and in the past few years he had made many mistakes and bad calls in his treatment of his wife; yet he still very much loved her. Not having her around allowed him to see just how lonely and miserable his life was without her. Attempting to get her back was not an option; he realized no matter what, he will get her back one way or another.

CHAPTER 15

THE TIES THAT BIND

O N A bright and sunny autumn Saturday morning, Taylor steps into the shower. Relaxing as the hot water rains down on her body. She closes her eyes and clears her mind.

Her tranquility is quickly interrupted when she hears footsteps outside of the shower. Her heart begins to race as fear takes hold. She calls out, "Who's there?" Nobody answers. She begins to wonder if she in fact was just hearing things. Suddenly the shower curtain is pulled away and there before her stands Alex, naked.

Taylor lets out a sigh of relief, remarking, "You startled me."

He steps inside the shower with her, "I thought I'd join you if that's alright," states Alex.

She turns to him, smiling, "Of course it is. If you wash my back, I'll wash yours."

He chuckles, "Oh, I'll do far more than wash your back."

Taylor kisses him passionately, "Didn't you tell me you were going back to London for a few days?"

Tilting his head to let the water run over his hair, he replies, "Yes, I have a meeting to attend there and then I'll be back. I was to leave tonight, but now due to the meeting being moved up two days, I won't leave until tomorrow. You know you could come with me. You have a passport now."

She smiles, "I'd love to but I can't leave the kids. I love my job. I look forward to going every day. Besides, once Christmas break is here, we'll go together and then I can meet your Mom and friends."

He smiles back at her, "Okay. I know for certain my mum can't wait to meet you. That's all I hear, 'when will I get to meet this lovely lady friend of yours?'"

Taylor moves closer to Alex's wet, naked body, hugging up to him, "That's nice."

Alex replies, "Don't be surprised when we come back married. She'll do her best to make it happen while we are visiting."

Taylor looks up at Alex, "She'll get no objections from me."

A look of wonderment crosses his face, "I was joking, but you're not. Does this mean if I were to ask you would say yes?" She shakes her head yes.

Alex kisses her passionately, holding her under the flow of the water. At that very same moment, at the end of the lane sitting in a rental car, Jonathan stares down towards the distant house, shielded by the trees.

On the phone, the detective gives him an additional update. "Your wife is in that house. She is living there with Mr. Parker and now has employment at a local elementary school where she is teaching kindergarten. A little bit of information I recently obtained is she has a new identity. Her name is now Beth Jones. This guy went to great lengths to keep you off their trail. From what I've been able to ascertain he is due back in London tomorrow, so he should be out of the house in order for you to retrieve your property." Jonathan hangs up the phone and gazes a moment longer at the house before driving away.

Later that day, Taylor begins cooking dinner, having given the maid and the cook the day off so she could make dinner for Alex before he leaves for London.

Alex wraps his arms around her from behind, "The smell in here is heavenly," says Alex.

Taylor chuckles, saying, "I haven't gotten far enough for it to smell heavenly."

Holding onto her tighter, he asks, "I was talking about you, not the food; so what can I do to help?"

"Absolutely nothing; I have everything under control. Dinner will be ready in about an hour. I'm going to slip upstairs when it is about finished and get ready for you. I want tonight to be very special, so you run along and find something to get into for a bit. I'll call you when it's ready," says Taylor.

Joyously Taylor prepares dinner, sets the table with china and candles. Slipping upstairs, while Alex sits at his desk dozing from drifting off while listening to a classical CD; she changes into a form fitting red dress with a matching sheer see-through blouse and heels.

Reentering the kitchen, oddly she notices the oven and stovetop are turned off, which she is certain is not how she left them. Thinking little of it, she turns to go after the plates on the table, when she is startled to see Jonathan standing quietly in the doorway, looking at her. She goes pale and begins to shake uncontrollably, as Jonathan says, "Hello, darling. Aren't you pleased to see me? I've missed you terribly."

Fearful of moving, she stands still, asking "Jonathan, how did you find me?"

He begins to slowly walk towards her, "You knew I'd find you. The truth of the matter is you could hide out anywhere and I'd find you one way or another. You know this of me. My question to you is why would you up and leave me making me go to such great lengths?"

Still fearing him yet trying her best to remain calm and rational, she continues talking, "I'm sorry. I just don't think we should be together anymore. You'll be much happier without me and I'm not good for you. You must see that."

Touching the side of her face, "I've been miserable without you. I can't and won't live without you. You're coming back with me," states Jonathan.

Tears well up in her eyes, as she quietly responds; "No, I won't go with you. I'm staying here."

Jonathan smirks, "So, you'd rather stay here with your British lover than with me?"

Suddenly it dawns on Taylor, that Alex is in the house and fearful of what Jonathan may have done, she pleads, "Jonathan, where is Alex? What have you done with him?"

Jonathan places his arm around Taylor, "Oh, he's fine. You'll see him again before we leave. I assure you, he is safe."

As he leads her towards the front entrance way, Taylor begins screaming for Alex, she races towards the stairs. Jonathan latches onto her by the hair, pulling her back. Pressing his mouth against her ear; he whispers, "Are you so intent on seeing your lover? I'll take you to him. I wouldn't want to keep you two apart for long."

Taking her upstairs to the master bedroom, the room is dark and quiet. Taylor scans the room frantically for any sign of Alex until finally she catches a glimpse of him in the corner near the bed, tied to a chair, with a gag in his mouth.

His eyes widen as he sees Jonathan holding onto her. Quickly he wiggles and squirms in an attempt to free himself. Jonathan speaks harshly to him, "Mr. Parker, if you love my wife you'll stop what you're doing. I have a gun and I'll kill her right here, right now. She'll be a part of you once I blow her brains all over you."

Alex sits still, watching as Jonathan turns a small bedside lamp on and pulls out a gun, holding it towards Taylor demanding she lay on the bed. He hands her a long white piece of rope, "Tie your left arm to the bedpost or I'll shoot him," Jonathan demands.

He points the gun at Alex. Taylor begins to cry as she does her best to tie her one arm to the bed, begging to Jonathan, "Please, Jonathan, don't do this. I'll leave with you right now. Things will go back to the way they were, I promise."

Jonathan cautiously moves to the other side of the bed, watching Alex as he passes in front of him. Taking another piece of rope he ties Taylor's free wrist to the other post and does the same with her ankles, leaving enough play in the ankle ropes.

Jonathan looks sternly at Alex, pointing his gun, he says, "I want you to have a good sense of what it's like to watch someone you love be taken by someone else, and to know that person is making love to the one person you treasure most."

Laying the gun on the bedside table across from Alex, he moves to the bottom of the bed, unfastening his pants. Taylor screams at him, "No, Jonathan! Please don't. I'm sorry—don't do this!" He ignores her pleas, pulling her down towards the end of the bed; ripping her dress off, exposing her naked body.

Alex pulls at the tied down chair, attempting to pull it away from its imprisoned position. Jonathan ignores him, quickly thrusting himself into his bound wife, who lies helplessly underneath him. Her cries cease, her tears stop and as her eyes turn and meet Alex he sees her death in that moment, knowing the pain which her husband has just inflicted has done what no gun could.

Her eyes stare over at him with emptiness. She doesn't fight, struggle or make any movements as Jonathan sexually assaults her. Tears roll down Alex's face as he helplessly looks at the one person he loves the most, whom he can't aid or protect from the one person he swore he would not allow to harm her.

Feverishly, Alex works the tie around his wrist, struggling to free his hands. Jonathan stands up, pulling his pants back up gasping to catch his breath. Taylor doesn't move. Jonathan begins to feel remorse for his actions as he looks at her naked body. Taking a cover he tosses it over her body.

He begins to cry as he struggles with what he considers to be a pending outcome. Laying down next to Taylor, as she continues gazing over at Alex in the opposite direction; Jonathan brushes her hair away from her face, saying emotionally, "I'm sorry, Taylor. I never wanted to hurt you. I only wanted you to love me and never leave me, yet you did leave me."

With his mouth resting closely to her right ear, he continues, "There are ties in life that cannot be broken, the ties that bind us together forever. I've gone over this in my head time and time again. I know there is no use in us going on, nor in my bringing you back with me. I know you no longer love me and in part I know that's my fault. However, I can't leave here allowing you to make a new life with this guy. I never thought I'd do this. I can't live without you, yet more so I can't let you live without me."

Jonathan kisses Taylor on the cheek before getting off the bed to walk over to retrieve the gun from the bedside table. Alex manages to free one hand, quickly lunging forward grabbing Jonathan's wrist, wrestling for the gun. A fierce power struggle ensues as Jonathan attempts to overpower Alex.

In one swift motion he knocks Alex to the floor breaking the antique chair in half, as Taylor is able to hear them scuffling on the floor. Suddenly a single shot rings out, her heart races. Moments later, Alex is able to struggle his other hand free to push Jonathan's limp body off of him.

Alex quickly unties his ankles from the chair and rushes to Taylor's side, frantically untying her wrists and ankles. Tears roll down his face as he scoops her up into his arms, rocking back and fourth with her, his voice quivers, "Taylor, I'm sorry. I'm so sorry. Please forgive me."

Her voice breaks weary and weak, "Is Jonathan dead?"

Alex responds, "Yes, I shot him in the chest. He will never hurt you ever again." She holds tightly to Alex. He holds to her tightly, rocking her back and fourth. She buries her face in his shirt, crying helplessly.

EPILOGUE

ALEX PUTS the plantation estate on the market. Neither he nor Taylor can find the beauty or luster any longer in a house that holds such a haunting and unforgettable reminder of the evil that threatened them both.

As the limousine pulls up to take them to the airport, Taylor rests her head on Alex's shoulder, holding to him tightly. He kisses her forehead and reassures her as they drive away from the house, "I'll make you happy and I know you'll rediscover who you are, finding a day where you have no more fears of the past," assures Alex.

Months pass as the two settle in a newly acquired estate in London. Taylor becomes more like herself and begins working again, now teaching pre-school and making new friends.

After becoming ill, Taylor fights off the flu, hoping to be better before the upcoming work week; however, after having difficulties keeping food down, Alex insists the family doctor pay a house call just to make certain all is well.

After a lengthy meeting, he races home to see how the patient is feeling. The doctor leaves the room upon his arrival, "How is she Dr. Atkins? Is it the flu that's going around?" asks Alex.

The doctor adjusts his glasses, looking at him in a serious nature, "Mr. Parker, the flu isn't going around. Taylor is suffering from morning sickness. She is pregnant."

Alex appears weak in the knees as if he may fall down at any given moment. The doctor grabs his arm and sits him down outside the door, asking "Mr. Parker, are you feeling alright?"

Shaking off the lightness in his head, Alex replies, "Yes. I'm just wonderful! How is she? Can I see her?"

The doctor laughs, "She's fine, she's resting. I gave her something to help with the nausea. She'll need to come in when she's feeling better for a full check up, just to make sure all is well. I'm guessing from things she isn't far along, maybe a couple of weeks. Give me a call if she gets to feeling worse. Have her attempt to eat something later. Good day, Mr. Parker."

Alex sits at the foot of the bed, smiling brightly at her. She smiles back, "I take it you've heard the news?"

Unable to control his excitement, he rushes to her bedside, "I do, how are you feeling?"

She sits up in bed, smiling with a luminous light in her eyes, "I'm feeling a lot better. How do you feel about becoming a father?"

Alex grins, "I've been patiently waiting and now I don't have to wait too much longer. I love you and couldn't be happier that you're carrying my child. We've had a rough go of things but now that is all behind us. I want you to be the mother of my children and my wife."

Taylor smiles, looking quizzically at Alex, "Alex, are you asking or just stating a general comment?"

He gets down on one knee, "I'm asking. Taylor, will you marry me. Will you become my wife?"

Her eyes sparkle, as she happily replies, "Yes, Alex Parker, I will marry you."

What was once a dream an unobtainable vision; now with Alex, all Taylor's dreams were one by one finally coming true. All the heartaches and turmoil were behind her, with only blue skies to pass her by.